Last Stand at Rio Blanco

Terrell L Bowers

DEDICATION

For my Mother-in-law, Burdie Jenkins, who became my strongest and most loyal supporter.

Chapter One

The scent of dried blood was carried by the afternoon breeze. And the sound of flies buzzing nosily attracted Trace McCain to the brush-covered ravine. He paused, turning slowing in his saddle to search the patches of mesquite and buckbrush. With fresh Indian sign discovered nearby two days before, it wouldn't do to make hasty appearances over hilltops. If he ran into some Apaches, he wanted the surprise to be on his side – not theirs.

He watched a rock wren flutter from salt brush to sage a hundred yards up the wash. A Chipmunk scurried up the gnarled branch of a downed smoke tree, spotted Trace on his horse, and froze in position. He switched his tail as if he were chasing off flies, and hastily turned and scrambled back down the branch, lost from sight almost instantly.

Seeing and hearing nothing more, Trace nudged his horse carefully up the crest of the wash. With his hand resting on his gun butt, he topped the rise and stopped.

The carcass of the steer was easily recognizable, for only the hindquarters were missing. The animal had been butchered in the low hollow, surrounded by trees and brush on all sides. It hadn't been lying there long – possibly an hour, according to trace's estimation. There were no human tracks visible in all of the blood-soaked grass. But the beef had been felled by two arrows, and the shafts still protruded from the steer's chest. There could be little doubt that the Indians had paid the Circle M ranch a visit.

Scouting in a short circle, Trace located two sets of footprints. As the Indians were on foot, they had to carry about eighty to a hundred pounds of beef. It would be slow going for them, so he should be able to overtake them before they reached the relative safety of the foothills. It wasn't an easy decision. For if he left the rest of the steer, it would be ruined meat. Nevertheless, he couldn't let the Indians get away with butchering one of the McCain animals, or they would be back. Word would spread that the Circle M was easy pickings.'

Pulling his .44 Henry from its scabbard, Trace started his mount towards the opposite side of the ravine. It would be hot, dry work, carrying that much beef over any great distance.

Those bucks would be bound to stop long enough to drink at the river, and might even follow the waterway right up to the mouth of the canyon. If he rode a straight line towards the foothills, he could cut them off and be waiting to greet them.

The sun was high in the sky, the midsummer heat growing in intensity as the afternoon wore on. Before Trace had gone two miles, the horse was lathered with sweat. He had to slow down to a walk often to keep the animal from giving out, and he began to fear he might not be able to get ahead of the braves.

The 'river' was a combination of three smaller streams from the mountains, all funneling down from different ranges, each adding it's trickle to the flow. The water level ran high after a storm or in the rainy season, but most of the time it was only a small stream. During the heat of summer, it ran about two- to three-feet deep in most places, and spanned fifteen to twenty feet across. Not what Trace would have considered to be a river, but that's what everyone called it – White River.

Heading towards the waterway, he slowed to a wary pace, keeping in the thick of the trees and brush for cover. He tightened his grip on the stock of his rifle as the water came into view. The bank was lined with grass and a scatter of trees and shrubs.

He paused to check for any sign, stopping his horse a full eighty yards from the bank of the waterway, letting his eyes wander in a slow, intense scrutiny. He was ahead of them – he felt it in his bones.

From his position, Trace was high enough to follow the winding course of the river – the boundary between the McCain Circle M ranch and Kendall's neighboring Double K ranch – for a solid mile. Beyond the borders of the two large spreads lay the town of Rio Blanco and the valley's flat grasslands. He could observe the area for a half mile to either side of the river, and there was no movement, not even the stirring of a dust devil.

Slowly his peruse rested upon the foliage that lined the banks of the river. Something moved. They were there, beneath the cover of the thick trees and dense underbrush, coming right up the river, walking right into the sights of his rifle. They would turn from the waterway when it took a sharp bend towards the upper southern hills, for the hills would put them almost in Mexico. Unless they wanted to head for the massive Sierra Madre mountains, they would turn towards him and right into his field of fire.

Trace about allowed himself a satisfied smile when he spotted something else moving near the bend in the river. He stared hard in that direction, picking out a point of interest for a marker. Then he pulled a pair of filed glasses out of his saddlebag and took a closer look. He found the marker quickly, then dropped the powerful lenses to a dark spot among the trees. It was big – too big to be a deer – and it was brown. And it was saddled!

'For the love of – ' he swore under his breath. There was someone down at the water's edge, likely a fisherman. He was going to pay a high price for any fish he caught. Unless he saw the Indians first, he would soon be a dead man.

Making a hasty decision, Trace neck-reined his horse down the slope, pointing him to the tethered animal. He stowed his glasses away and readied his Henry, taking time to jack a shell into the chamber.

How quickly the pattern of the hunt had changed. Now he was forced to risk exposure by entering the heavy brush. He dipped beneath the shadow of the trees, following a worn animal trail that was used by wildlife and cattle alike.

He tired to keep his horse quiet, but he feared there was little time left. He would have no advance warning if the Indians simply slipped past the fisherman. If he blundered into them blindly, his chances were less than even, not exactly the way he'd planned things a few minutes before. He'd held the high ground, had surprise on his side, plus he would have gotten off the first shot. His chances of getting both braves was good. Presently, it was a toss-up.

Moving steadily closer to the water, Trace stopped his horse every few steps, listening for any sounds – especially those of approaching feet. It was impossible to penetrate the dense brush enough to see what lay ahead. He pushed forward a short way, then suddenly jerked his animal to a halt. He thought the sound of the water was wrong, as if someone were thrashing about in the river ....

An ear-piercing scream shattered the stillness, the terror-stricken cry of a woman! While the water was still hidden by the trees and shrubs, Trace knew she wasn't more than twenty yards away.

He swung his right leg over the horn of the saddle and jumped to the ground. Then he dashed quickly through the undergrowth, not wanting to alert the Indians to his coming, yet rushing forward to prevent them harming or killing the woman.

A second cry echoed through the afternoon serenity. He took advantage of it, tugging through a stand of wild currant to reach the shore. He continued along the water's edge and saw a flash of human bodies in a deathlike struggle, smack in the middle of the creek.

A girl was splashing around, half submerged by one Indian's strong hands. He held her head under water, until she managed to twist from his grasp. She gasped for air, flailing about with both hands, trying to beat off her assailant. His long black hair was held in place by a band around his head, his white cotton shirt and loincloth soaked from the battle. White paint ran from one side of his face to the other, across his nose, which added to the hideous sneer that contorted his features. He hissed a curse as the girl raked his cheek and shoulder with her fingernails.

The young woman was clad only in a chemise of sorts, having obviously been bathing when surprised by the two braves. Currently, she was fighting for her life, clawing, hitting, biting -- frantic to escape from the deadly savage.

Trace frantically scanned the wall of trees and brush. Where was the second Indian?

Another horrified exclamation from the girl caused him to look back at her struggle. The Indian had a firm grip on her hair with one hand, and he had pulled a deadly looking knife. He was poised to slash with the gleaming blade – raised up in the air, preparing to strike!

Trace had no choice. He threw the Henry to his shoulder and fired, all in a single motion. The bullet struck the man squarely in the chest. He took a backward step and the knife sailed harmlessly out of his hand. He toppled over into the water and was immediately swept along in the gentle current.

Trace instinctively ducked, for he still had no idea where the second Indian was at. His sudden move saved his life. An arrow swished past his head, sinking its tip into a nearby tree. The girl cried out, 'over there!' and pointed to the far bank of the river.

Without hesitation, Trace spun in that direction, levering another shell into his rifle as he did so. He aligned the sights on the Indian as the Apache drew back a second arrow in his bow. Trace pulled the trigger an instant before the brave could launch a second shot.

Through the puff of smoke from the end of his rifle, Trace saw the Indian disappear. He stood there a moment, ejecting the spent casing and shoving a fresh round into the chamber. Then he waded across the river, ready to lash out with the gun or take another shot if needed.

Entering the tall grass along the bank, he discovered the Indian warrior, but he was no longer a threat. Trace's bullet had killed him outright. Considering how fast he had fired, he knew he'd been lucky to have scored a mortal hit.

'D-did you get him?' the girl's timid voice asked in little more than a whisper.

Trace pivoted in her direction. She was still standing in the middle of the river, drenched and shivering. Her long dark-brown hair was pasted to her scalp and clung to her shoulders. A trickle of blood seeped from a cut at the corner of her mouth and he perceived a bruise above one eye. She had put up one heck of a fight.

'These two won't be killing any more beef or terrorizing unsuspecting bathers.'

The girl's eyes searched the water near her and focused on the floating body of the other Indian. The gentle flow had moved his body about ten feet.

'They – he was going to kill me,' she said, incredulously. 'I wasn't doing anything to hurt them, and yet they would have killed me.'

'You're a white woman,' Trace said. 'Anyone with our color of skin is their enemy ... whether we feel the same about them or not. Can't reason with an Apache.'

As he spoke, he walked along the shoreline until he located the girl's riding skirt and blouse. They had been hanging over a small shrub. Her boots and hat were sitting next to them.

'You'd best be getting dressed, miss,' he said, bobbing his head at her outfit. 'Someone might have heard the shooting. I'll pull that warrior from the creek before he fouls the water.'

The girl looked uncertainly at Trace, waiting until he waded into the water before she hurried to the shore. He ignored her as best he could, having his hands full with the water-soaked Indian. Though he could hear the rustle of her skirt, he didn't look in her direction. By the time he'd dragged and laid out the two braves in one spot, she had donned her clothes.

Trace rolled the two men into a runoff ditch and kicked some dirt and rocks over their bodies. He felt the girl's eyes on his back as he finished the hasty chore. When he rotated about to meet her, he found a perplexed look etched in her face.

'I know you,' she said. 'You're one of the McCains.'

He sensed the coolness and hostility in her voice, as if saying his name repulsed her. He regarded her with a critical eye, appraising her from head to foot. She cringed inwardly at his candid inspection, but held her chin high and her back remained rigid with a mustered bravado.

'Yes, I'm a McCain,' he admitted. 'Trace McCain.'

She swallowed, forcing herself to meet his eyes with a level gaze. Clearly, she had some grit.

'I was lucky that you happened along,' she said, displaying some grace, after a short pause. 'You saved my life.'

'It wasn't luck, my saving your life,' he corrected her.

'No?'

'I was sitting at the top of the ravine, waiting for these two jaspers to come out of the trees. They killed one of our steers back down the trail a bit. I was tracking them when I spotted your horse.'

The girl's cheeks flushed slightly. 'Is that all you saw?'

Trace allowed himself a thin smile. 'I'm afraid so, miss. There wasn't time to take in any scenery, once you started screaming.'

'Father always told me that if I couldn't fight, I'd better learn to scream real loud. The advice seems to have paid off.'

'Yup,' he said. 'I imagine they heard you all the way up at your ranch house.'

'I'm glad you were closer than that,' she told him, showing a bit more gratitude. 'I wasn't fairing so well in my fight against the Indian. He was about to take my scalp.'

'You're quite a piece from your house,' he said critically. 'I shouldn't think you would be this far away from help. There are a number of wandering Indians about, and white women are one of their favorite targets.'

She tipped her head toward the slight curve in the creek. 'The water is deep and still there at the bend. It makes a nice pool for bathing.'

'It does look inviting,' Trace said. 'But I can't imagine your father allowing you to go so far from your ranch house to wash.'

'He doesn't know that I come here. Father's warned me many times to stay away from the river – not because of Indians, but because of your family.'

Trace laughed without humor. 'Well, it's nice to know we're regarded as highly as the Apaches.'

'Your father killed my Uncle Randolph.'

'He was hanged for it,' Trace replied. 'We boys had no hand in the fight, or the cause behind it.'

'Your father attacked my aunt. Randolph was protecting her.'

'My old man was a hound dog,' Trace admitted the truth. 'My mother knew it when she married him, but she had no choice but to stick by him. We boys were on the wild side, but we never hurt anyone. Yet everyone in the valley holds us responsible for what our Pa did.'

'My brother, Randy, was named after my uncle,' the girl said. 'And Aunt May had to return to her family back in Ohio. She was too ashamed to stay in the valley.'

Trace sighed. 'You ever think maybe she left because of guilt?'

'Of course. She felt bad having been the cause of the deaths of two men.'

Trace could see the girl had no clue about the real circumstances, but he let it go. The quick trial and hanging of their father had left little doubt as to the story given at the time. Plus, the truth had no bearing on the outcome.

'You better get on home,' he said. 'If someone from your ranch caught us together, I could end up hanging from one of these taller trees.'

'I wouldn't allow that,' the girl said with some spunk. 'You McCains have a right to run your ranch, the same as you are allowed to shop at the general store in town. No one holds you personally responsible for the actions of your father.'

'They just hate us for the fun of it, huh?'

'Your ranch covers several miles, including a lot of good bottomland. The soil along that stretch could support a dozen families.'

'Hence the reason the farmers don't like us.'

'A lot of them are scratching for a meager existence on rocky or clay soil. Naturally, they are going to envy your holdings.'

'We bought the property, legally,' Trace said. 'We use the bottomland to raise hay for the dry seasons.'

She started to walk toward her horse but stopped and looked back over her shoulder. 'I won't forget that you saved my life,' she said quietly. 'I can't take your side against the other people in the valley, but I will tell anyone who asks that you are an excellent shot ... and a gentleman.'

He grinned. 'Thank you, for the kind words, miss.'

'The name is Melanie Kendall,' she said. 'But I'm sure you knew that already.'

'Keep a careful watch, Miss Kendall,' he warned, not responding to her statement. 'Charo cut sign of these two Indians a couple days back. We haven't seen any others, but there might be more of them around.'

'Father is more concerned about a gang of raiders.'

'Raiders?'

'We received word that a large band of cutthroats are attacking the settlements along the border. As you know, ever since the end of the war, we've had very little support from the army or the law against robbers and bandits.'

'Rio Blanco would be easy pickings for a gang of any size,' Trace agreed.

'They rob the little towns or steal the cattle from the ranchers and sell the goods or beef on both sides of the border. Often they have several Indians riding with them.'

'Sounds like something we all need to worry about.'

'We only have about half as many men as we need on our ranch. I don't think we would fare very well against the raiders.'

'Yeah, we're not long of firepower ourselves, except for Charo and myself.'

The girl tucked her damp hair under the edge of her hat, then climbed aboard her horse. Rather than speak again, she raised a hand in farewell and headed her mount in the direction of her ranch.

Trace wished he knew how to remove the barrier between his family and most everyone in the valley. But the man his father had killed was more than just a resident, he had been a well-respected man within the community. The sins of their father had tainted the rest of the McCains.

Once the girl was gone, Trace hunted around and discovered the quarter of beef. He strapped the meat over the back of his horse and headed for home.

As he threaded his way back to the main trail, he couldn't get his mind off of the girl, nor the warm feeling her look of gratitude ignited within his chest. He had seen hostility in her first expression, but he felt he had knocked a rail or two off of the fence between them after talking to her.

Melanie seemed intelligent, although still biased against the McCains for the loss of her uncle. Plus, Charo had done little to mend fences between the townsfolk and their family. He had a quick temper and a quicker gun, making them even more unwanted. As for the remainder of the boys, Lonnie, Bud and Dean had never been in any trouble. Dean had married a local widow, and the four other boys should have been welcomed – what with the war taking many of the young men from the valley. But their father had put a hex on the boys. Killing Randolph had not been forgotten or forgiven, even after John McCain was hanged for the crime.

The sun was at its height, blistering the sand and canyon walls, but Trace was used to the hot Texas weather. He wondered about the raiders Melanie had spoke of. If they came looking for beef or an easy town to ransack, Rio Blanco would look quite inviting.

Reaching the trail to the McCain ranch, Trace could not prevent a melancholy from entering his being. Previously, he had seen Melanie from a distance, but had never spoken to her. Now, recalling the girl, dressed in an almost transparent bit of underclothing, wet and shivering, with her arms crossed and her hair pasted to her head ... the vision was ingrained in his mind's eye. He had purposely tried not to stare at her, while she was so exposed and helpless. But he couldn't stop the yearning feeling, the desire to be something more than a member of the family her father and brother hated.

'Get your head on straight!' Trace muttered to himself. 'You've got about as much chance of winning over that gal as you do to grow a third arm!'

Chapter Two

Sod McCain stood near the rock fireplace, his elbow on the mantel. Being the senior member of the McCain family, he had aged considerably since his son was hanged. He made no excuses for John, who was his only son, but his death had caused him a great deal of pain. His whitish hair was neatly trimmed around his neck, but several locks dangled onto his forehead. He was weathered with age, his face lined with creases, tanned from the sun, yet as resilient as shoe leather. He was the smallest man in the room, standing an inch shorter than Bud, who might still have a final growth spurt before he left his final teenage year behind. Sod was the indisputable ramrod of the Circle M ranch, and he swept a intense gaze over his five grandsons, who were assembled in the room.

'Sit down, boys,' he said in his mild voice. 'We've some palavering to do.'

Dean was already seated on the couch, so young Bud joined him there. Ever-restless Charo leaned against the wall, Lonnie plopped down on the arm of the couch, and Trace relaxed in one of the room's two easy chairs. Sod waited for them to get comfortable before he spoke again.

'Trace ran across a couple Apaches today,' he began. 'They downed a steer in an arroyo, this side of the river. He followed them and killed them both.'

'Way to go, Trace!' Charo approved. 'Two less renegades to worry about.'

Sod nodded his agreement, but it was not what he wanted to

expound upon. 'Trace also encountered the Kendall girl at the river,' he continued. 'She told him about an outlaw gang – running with a few Indians – that has been causing a lot of grief west of here. They started out doing some rustling, but they have moved up to looting and robbing some of the smaller towns.

'Stoco mentioned something about those raiders, Gramps,' Dean contributed.

'What did he say?' Sod asked.

Dean's expression was serious. 'He said they are the gang that attacked Little Bend a few weeks back.'

The old man folded his arms in thought. 'Reckon the gal was telling you straight, Trace.'

'I don't doubt she believed the rumor,' he replied. 'If it had been her old man talking, I'd have been uncertain if the pair of braves I killed were even Indians.'

'Yep, Kendall won't ever forgive us for my son killing his brother. I'm surprised the girl even spoke to you.'

'The two Indians were fixing to cause her some grief,' Trace told him. 'It was fortunate for her I arrived when I did.'

'I've never seen her close up. Is she pretty?' Lonnie asked.

'Like a bald-faced heifer,' Trace lied. 'You better stick with the Banning girl you've been sneaking out to visit on Sunday afternoons.'

That brought a laugh from the other boys in the room. Lonnie had been trying to hide his clandestine meetings with the young lady, but there were few secrets in the McCain family.

'Let's stay on point here,' Sod said, taking some of the heat off of the second youngest McCain boy – though twenty-two was hardly a boy.

'Way I see it,' Dean put in, 'we need to hire more help. Our three men and us can't protect the entire herd.'

'Dean's right,' Charo agreed. 'We've got fences that need repair, and our holding corrals and branding chutes are falling down from use. There isn't time for us to get everything done.'

'I'm in full agreement with you,' Sod confirmed. 'But where do we get the men? There has been so much confusion and crooked goings on with the government since the end of the war, that all of Texas is short of able lawmen.'

'I reckon there's some good men to be had in El Paso. We could recruit a few of them. A good many of the ex-Confederates are still searching for steady work.'

'That's probably whose running the gang of cutthroats,' Lonnie said. 'Ex-Confederates!'

Sod gave a nod. 'It's true that we have quite a few discontented ex-soldiers who have taken to the outlaw trail. But the *who* is not the worry, it's the *when* will they come to Rio Blanco?'

Trace took the floor. 'Even if we were to send someone to hire help from El Paso, it would take a week or two. If we get hit before then, we would miss that extra gun.'

'Gramps could go,' Charo volunteered. 'He's the worst shot in the family – not even barring the women.'

Sod frowned. 'I think I can outshoot your ma.'

'Don't let her hear you say that,' Charo chuckled, 'or we'll have a contest on our hands.'

'I've got five dollars on Mom,' Buddy chirped gleefully. 'Any takers?'

'Very funny, Bud,' the old man grunted. 'It's plain to see John never boxed your ears enough whilst you were growing up.'

'He was too busy chasing other men's wives,' Dean said, unable to keep the anger from his voice.

Sod didn't defend his son. Instead, he returned to the problem at hand. 'As you young stallions don't seem to need me, I'll ride over to El Paso and hire several men. As for the rest of you, we need to set up some kind of signal. If trouble comes before I return, you need to be ready.'

'We can have Stoco, Benez and Franciso take turns watching from Eagle's Point,' Trace suggested. 'They can send up smoke if they see a bunch of riders heading this way.'

'Meanwhile,' Dean joined in with the plan, 'we can push the herd over to the east pastures and north canyon. That way we can protect them.'

'I'll leave first thing in the morning,' Sod decided. He pointed a finger at Trace. 'Until you get the sentry on Eagle's Point, you and Bud should take turns keeping watch. Everyone else stay close to the house, except when moving the cattle.'

'How about the dance tomorrow night?' Lonnie asked.

Dean harrumphed. 'You sure you want to bring your courtship out into the open?'

'There will be trouble,' Charo put in. 'You know the McCain haters will be looking for a chance to fix your wagon.'

Lonnie scowled, his jaw rigid. 'I'm sick of being treated like we were dirt. Pa did what he did, but he paid for it! A death for a death! I've been sneaking around with Tish for several months now, and it's time we let the people know how we feel.'

'I figured to tag along,' Trace said quietly. 'If there's enough of us, maybe no one will start any trouble.'

'Count me in too!' Charo volunteered. 'We've been backing away long enough. If there's going to be trouble, let's get to it!'

Dean didn't argue, but looked at Sod. 'What do you say, Gramps?'

Sod obviously didn't want to provoke a fight, especially with the chance the people would need to stand together if the raiders showed up. Even so, he gave a reluctant nod of approval.

'I reckon this needs to be settled, one way or the other, and putting it off sure hasn't done anything to ease the hatred.'

'We'll all go,' Dean announced. 'Lora hasn't been dancing since we were married, and this is our valley, our town too. We'll avoid a fight as best we can, but we will go as a complete family ... in case there is trouble.'

The adobe ranch house was as good as a fort, solid, nearly bullet-proof, and resistant to fire, except for the roof. The windows had two-inch cedar shutters that could be closed, allowing only a small opening for rifles. The McCains had never met the man who built the place, but it had been constructed with the knowledge that Indian territory was only a short ride away. Every safety feature had been thought out in advance.

There were no nearby trees, rock formations, or gullies to hide or fight from. The area approaching the ranch was open in all directions for nearly a hundred yards – except for a few pinyon and a spot or two of sagebrush. The only other buildings were the bunkhouse, barn, and a shelter in the corner of the two corrals. There was a trap door in the roof of the main house, and the walls extended up like castle battlements. Several men could hold off a small army from the roof.

With the house fairly secure from attack, it was the cattle that worried the McCains. They could put them in the box canyon or on the farthest pastures, but to protect them would take men – something they were short of. If the raiders attempted to steal the cattle, it would be a long-running fight, one in which the odds didn't favor the McCains.

The next morning Trace and Dean outlined the plans, both knowing the importance of every man's task, and each of them able to run the ranch if something should happen to the other. They compared notes on whom to put where if a fight came and how to relay warnings.

It was complicated and they spent an hour coming up with a suitable plan. They finished over coffee with Lora joining them.

'I don't think we should go to the dance tonight,' Lora said when the two men had grown silent. 'It seems to me the timing is bad, what with the worry about this gang of outlaws.'

'Lonnie has made up his mind,' Trace said. 'You and Dean don't have to attend.'

'There will be trouble,' she insisted. 'Tish Banning's brother, Lex, thinks of himself as her guardian since their folks died of cholera some years back. He won't allow the two of them to dance together. He is very outspoken and is always trying to start a fight.'

'We'll try and avoid trouble,' Trace assured her, 'but it's time people realized that we're here to stay. Pa did what he did, but he paid the price. None of us knew what he was up to those nights he went off drinking and chasing skirts. We aren't responsible for his actions, any more than the Kendalls are responsible for the actions of Randolph's wife.'

'Trace is right, honey,' Dean said gently. 'If we don't quit backing away, these people will try and push us clear out of the valley. We have to draw the line. Those who cross that line, if they come toting iron or carrying a noose, will find we McCains are not afraid of them.'

Lora could see the men had made up their minds. With a sigh, she said: 'I thought I would wear my yellow-and-white go-to-meeting gown. Will that be suitable?'

Dean smiled warmly at the hard-working, destitute widow he had married – shortly before John McCain got himself hanged. 'You'll stand them on their ear,' he said.

'Or knock them on it, huh, Trace?' she asked her brother-in-law.

'Maybe both,' he said, displaying a grin. 'You be sure to save a dance for me – likely be the only dance I get.'

'I presumed you would be hot on the heels of the Kendall girl,' she said.

'Trace compared her to a cow,' Lonnie remarked. 'Why should he want to take up with her? There are a dozen gals around town who aren't hard on the eyes, and he'd be the right age for most of them.'

Lora raised her eyebrows. 'You called Melanie Kendall a cow?'

The room was suddenly hot and uncomfortable to Trace. He swallowed the tightness in his throat. 'Well, I was trying not to … '

'You mean she's pretty?' Dean queried. 'I've never met her before, only her brother and father.'

'If you would accompany Mom and me to church, you would have seen her for yourself.'

'I told you before,' Dean complained, 'my being there would likely caused a fight. The people are more polite to you two than any of us boys.'

'Yes, I know,' Lora conceded. 'To clarify, let me say that Melanie is not a girl anyone would call plain or unattractive. She's as pretty as any girl in the country.'

Dean eyed Trace with open suspicion. 'What was she doing at the river, Trace? You didn't say how she was involved in your fight with the two Indians.'

Trace heaved a sigh. 'She was getting manhandled by one of the bucks. I kind of saved her life.'

'Kind of?' Lora wanted a better explanation. 'How does one *kind of* save a person's life?'

'The brave was about to take her hair – all right!' he said with some force. 'I didn't want the whole family thinking – '

'Thinking what?' Lora cut in. 'That you saved the life of a girl who probably hates us for killing her uncle?'

'Ah-hah!' Dean laughed out loud. 'That ought to frost old man Kindell's whiskers! His precious daughter is saved by a McCain!'

'Dean!' Lora snapped at her husband. 'Show a little restraint.'

He gave her a surprised look and she said: 'Can't you see this whole thing has Trace in an emotional turmoil?'

'Huh?' he said dumbly. 'An emotional turmoil? What are you talking about?'

'Any man would be proud as a peacock to have saved a pretty girl from being scalped. Yet Trace kept it to himself.'

'Uh,' Dean was still lost. 'So?'

'So leave him alone. If this act of heroism endears Trace to Melanie, that's a good thing for the whole family.'

'Sometimes I think you read too many of those female novels,' Dean said. 'Trace sure knows better than to go all soft and mushy on a girl that he can never have.' He looked at his brother. 'Isn't that right?'

'I wouldn't dare speak to her in public, if that's what you mean,' he snapped off his reply. 'In fact, the Kendall girl was the only reason I took the two Indians at the river. I was set up and waiting for them to show out in the open when I spotted her. Going to her aid could have gotten me killed.'

'None of that matters,' Dean said grinning, 'Old man Kendall is going to chew iron and spit nails when he finds out.'

'This could still be a big step in settling the feud,' Lora said hopefully.

Trace grunted. 'I wouldn't slap away an offered handshake, but I don't expect it … not from that cantankerous old bear.'

'I expect you're right,' Dean said. 'He's got a hate that won't quit. Randolph and him were about as close as a double-yoke egg. I doubt he'll give up his pent-up rage, not even with you saving his daughter from the Indians.'

***

The barn dance only took place two or three times a year. Not one of the McCains had attended one since John's hanging. This would be a first.

Trace fell in with Lonnie and Bud, following Dean and Lora in the carriage. The three riding behind the buggy were silent, a grim determination overshadowing any conversation.

Even Lonnie, who had to be excited about being seen with Tish for the first time in public, was quiet. He had no false expectations, no illusions of being left alone. He knew Trace and Charo would be there, although Charo was running late, having been herding cattle up the box canyon. Their only reason for going would be to stand by him if trouble started.

Even as the thought crossed Trace's mind, he knew he was lying to himself. He had combed his hair, shaved, and was wearing his only good jacket and trousers. His polished boots were as shined as when he had attended Dean's wedding, and it was not on behalf of young Lonnie, but on the chance he might meet up with Melanie again.

She would undoubtedly be present, and he rather hoped to get a word or two with her. Of course, her father would probably be there as well, so the chances of speaking to her would be slim at best. But a smile or wave would make the trip worthwhile. If it meant taking a beating, he could accept that too, but only after putting up as much defense as he could muster.

The parson's barn sat on the edge of town, and was also used for Sunday meetings. It was an enormous barn and was more dignified for church or other meetings than the saloon.. During the short trial for John McCain, it was also used as a courthouse. It is where he was sentenced to be hanged. Nowadays, Lora and Ma McCain went to Sunday meetings, but the men stayed away to avoid a fight.

Buckboards, wagons, and a considerable number of horses were tethered all about the barn. Music could be heard as the McCains entered the huge yard. Dean hitched his team as the others tied their mounts to hitch posts, shrubs or wherever they could. It was going to be a full house.

Lora lifted her long skirt and petticoats to step down from the wagon. Both Dean and Trace were there to help her to the ground. Then they paused as a group until Bud and Lonnie joined them.

'Well,' Lonnie said, unable to conceal his dread.

'Yeah,' Trace joined his apprehension. 'Here we are.'

'Shall we go in?' Lora prompted them. 'I'm not going to dance out here in the dark.'

Dean took her arm and led the way. Trace fell in behind, with

Lonnie to one side and Bud to the other. Of the group, Trace was the tallest, and he outweighed all but Dean.

Dean was the eldest son; he also ate better due to having a wife and spending more time at home.

Lonnie was as wiry as Bud, even though he was three years older than the youngest of the McCain boys. He did most of the bookkeeping for the ranch, and had a history of being ill more than the others, often catching colds or bouts of fever. It might have had something to do with spending more time doing bookwork and not getting the same exercise as the others. Trace was the strongest physically and best marksman with a rifle of the five brothers, while Charo was a genuine wizard with a handgun.

As Trace followed Dean and Lora, he hoped that a brawl could be avoided, but he knew the odds were slim. There was too much animosity against their family. Someone would be sure to object to them attending the dance. Besides that, Lonnie would prompt a scandal when he danced with Tish Banning. Her brother, Lex, would never approve of the relationship, and he was a big-mouth bully. While he was too big and tough for Lonnie to handle, Trace figured he could match him in a fight. He sure didn't want to go toe-to-toe tonignt, but he was prepared, if forced into a corner.

Bales of straw were lined around the inner walls of the barn for people to use as benches. The floor itself was covered with a mixture of sawdust and straw for dancing. A table was set up with a large punch bowl and cups, along with a couple plates of cookies. The band comprised of four fellows playing instruments and one fellow calling out moves as the music played. As the McCains entered, there were a dozen or so couples square-dancing.

'Allemande Left,' the caller sounded off. 'Find your partner and swing her 'round!' He paused while the couples on the floor responded. 'Now everyone dosado.' Another pause: 'And grab your sweetheart and promanade ... '

'There's Tish!' Lonnie spoke up. 'Sitting there as beautiful as a prize rose in a garden of flowers!'

Trace saw her, sitting among three other unaccompanied ladies. He had to admire his brother's courage, as he walked right over to her. She rose to her feet to meet him and they joined hands.

Trace met the glares and open hostility with a cool passiveness. He wouldn't make the first move to cause any trouble.

A figure emerged from the spectators, just as the square-dancing music came to an end. The man approached and his badge showed on his vest. He wore no gun, was a bit shorter than Trace, and was about forty years of age.

Trace offered a peace-offering smile. 'How do, Sheriff Cod,' he greeted him. 'Been a spell since I last saw you.'

The sheriff stepped up close, his skeptical glance roaming over the other McCains.

'What's the idea, Trace?' he challenged, keeping his voice low enough so it didn't carry to any of the nearby people.

'This is a social dance, isn't it?' Trace replied. 'We're here to be sociable.'

'You promised me the last time you had a fight in town that you'd avoid any more trouble!'

'We didn't come for trouble, Barney,' Trace told him. 'We came to town to demonstrate that we are part of this community.'

The man bridled. 'Lex Banning is here tonight, and he's been drinking. Old man Kendall is here too. You're just the match to light the fuse to start a fight.'

Trace put a hard look on the sheriff. 'Look, Barney, there might be some trouble coming, but it won't be from us. What my father did was an unforgivable sin ... and he paid for his transgression with his life. None of us McCains had anything to do with what happened — it was all his doing. How much retribution do you and these other people need? You hanged him! Isn't that enough?'

'I'm not the one who will cause trouble, Trace. Your family being here will do that all by itself!'

Trace shook his head. 'If you want to curb trouble, talk to the troublemakers, not us. We won't be the ones who start anything.'

The sheriff pointed a bony finger at him. 'Dang it all, Trace! If these men take after you and your brothers, I won't get in their way.'

'Nice to know where the law stands, Barney. Have you picked out a skirt to hide behind, or do you intend to run outside and hide somewhere in the dark?'

Barney moved back a step, his face turning bright red. 'I'm warning you, Trace!'

'No!' Trace flared back. 'I'm warning you, Sheriff. If the law won't protect us, we will do it ourselves. Charo will be along shortly. Anyone who doesn't want us here can take it up with him!'

Those words had meaning. Charo had once demonstrated his ability to the townspeople in Rio Blanco. Five candles at ten paces, each of them burning, and Charo had put out three without hitting wax. He had not been showing off, he had been averting a gunfight with one of the locals.

'We don't want any gunplay, Trace,' the sheriff admitted quietly. 'I don't want to see anyone hurt.'

'Then you had best talk to the Kendalls and Lex Banning,' Trace warned. 'We're here to stay tonight – until we decide to leave.'

The sheriff had used his bluster and badge to try and cower or intimidate Trace, but it hadn't worked. He spun on his heel and disappeared back into the crowd. Trace figured it would probably be the last time he was seen for the night.

Barney wore the badge, but he wasn't much of a lawman. He had a bad knee, so he could hardly ride a horse, and to remain on his feet for more than a few hours was a hardship he didn't like to endure. He wore the badge only because he hadn't been physically fit to take on a regular job.

The music started again, a slow waltz tempo this time, with the fiddler, banjo picker and mouth-organ player trying to stay in time with the town's only piano. It was used in the Short-Horn Saloon all week, and for church meetings on Sundays – along with special occasions like the infrequent dances.

Trace hated to wear a gun at a dance, but if the odds were too great, he might need it before the night was over. He walked to the punch bowl and poured himself a cup. Then he took an unobtrusive position against the wall, being able to oversee most of the barn area while trying to not be too noticeable himself.

Lonnie was already dancing with Tish, and Dean had his wife out there enjoying the music too. Other than a few indignant stares, there was no break in the festivity.

The array of colors was dazzling, with reds and yellows predominant among the women's dresses. Trace enjoyed watching the swirl of petticoats, and the men looked like proper gentlemen, all decked out in the Sunday-best. Unfortunately, Lex Banning was among those in attendance, and he was not happy to see his sister with one of the dastardly McCains.

Trace kept an eye on him, concerned he was keeping company with Randy Kendall and one of the Double K hands, a man he knew on sight, but not by name.

Randy was talking in earnest to Lex, and it appeared to concern the McCains. As the two of them began the walk around the dance floor, Randy could not hide his limp. He had taken a nasty fall a couple years back and broke his leg. The doctor in town wasn't up to much and the limb had healed improperly, causing him a lot of trouble.

Lex took the lead, his arms swinging like some big ape, with a mug to match – thick lips, a protruding forehead, and hair abounded from every inch of flesh on the man. He had attempted to groom a mustache and beard, but it looked more like someone had shaved the hind end of a beaver and stuck on a couple black buttons for eyes.

Before they could make their way around to Trace, Charo entered the barn. He walked in as nonchalantly as if he would be welcomed by everyone present. He even tipped his hat to a couple of ladies, before removing it altogether. He sauntered over to the punch bowl, dipped himself a drink with a glass, then sashayed over to Trace.

'Looks like a humdinger of a dance,' he said. 'More pretty girls than I remembered.'

'It's a good turnout,' Trace agreed. 'Looks as if every man in the valley is here tonight.'

'You been out kicking up any straw yet?'

'Nope. I was waiting to see how many gals would turn you down first.'

Charo chuckled. 'Good idea. If they won't dance with me, it's a cinch they wouldn't dance with you.'

'Oh?'

'Take a look in the mirror some time,Trace. Ma always said that I was the best looking of the boys. If I was listing us in order of who was most handsome in the family, you'd be dead last … after the dog.'

'You're too kind,' Trace grunted. 'Remind me to turn my back if you get into trouble tonight. I'm sure Lonnie and Bud will be a lot of help.'

'OK, OK,' he said. 'I'll admit you are better looking than the hound dog, and you're not as skinny as Lonnie or Bud. I told Bud I had two job offers for him -- as a scarecrow.'

'And what did he tell you?'

Charo snorted. 'Ma would have washed his mouth out with a bar of lye soap if she'd have heard him. I didn't know Bud even knew some of those words.'

'Whatever he told you, it goes for me too.'

'All right, fair citizens of Rio Blanco,' the town parson spoke up from the bandstand. 'We've had time to see the men's choices for the dances so far. It's time to give the ladies a chance. Ladies, choose your partner for the next dance.' He laughed. 'And don't be afraid to get

Grandpa or one of the clumsy cowpokes who can't tell his left foot from his right. We'll make this a slow tune, so you can dodge having your toes stepped on.'

There was a mingling of bodies, people filing to the sides of the barn, others moving into the middle of the room. Trace did not pay much attention until someone approached him. He looked up to see a bright, smiling face.

'Trace McCain,' Melanie said gaily, 'if you refuse to dance with me, I'll cut the saddle cinch on your horse and you can walk home!'

'Ma'am – Miss Kendall?' he sputtered, rising to his feet. 'You're willing to dance with me?'

He quickly handed his glass of punch to Charo and accompanied Melanie to the main part of the dancing area.

The music started as they approached, so they fell in with the other people dancing at once. Trace threw a worried look for Harvey or Randy Kendall. They were bound to be outraged that Melanie should *ask* a McCain to dance – especially one who hadn't previously asked her for the same pleasure.

'Are you looking for someone?' Melanie asked, noticing his nervous gaze.

'Uh, no, Miss Kendall, I was just wondering … '

'You're supposed to pay attention to me,' she teased.

'I reckon most everyone in the place is paying attention to you,' he replied. 'Not only are you the prettiest gal here, but you've got more brass than a military band.'

Her bright eyes lifted to study him. 'Hum … ' she said with a thoughtful expression. 'I heard a rumor that you compared me to a cow.'

Trace felt as mortified as if his pants had just fallen around his ankles. He gulped ignominiously, trying to recover enough bravado to squeak out a response. 'W-who … ' was the only word he could get to pass through his lips.

'Tish is a friend of mine,' she said. 'Lonnie told her ... she told me ... I told you,' she explained. 'It's called gossip ... and I am always eager to hear what's said about me.'

He groaned. 'So you asked me to dance, figuring it would be a good way to teach me a lesson?'

She laughed. 'From the color in your cheeks, I'd say I more than got even.'

'I only made the statement to keep from being roasted alive by my brothers,' Trace admitted. 'I can see now, it was a big mistake. Far better to take a dressing down from them than from you.'

'Well,' Melanie chirped. 'You didn't say what kind of cow. Some are quite charming.'

'It would definitely be a Jersey,' Trace said quickly. 'They have the prettiest eyes and the best disposition of any cattle I was ever around.'

'A milk cow,' she said. 'I recall Father telling me they also give the richest milk.'

Trace swallowed the lump of humble pie and shook his head. 'I do apologize, Miss Kendall. I would die before I would ever intentionally insult you.'

'You don't strike me as being afraid of anything, yet you are afraid of me? Of women?'

'Not afraid exactly,' he fought back. 'It's more of a respect for something I don't fully understand.'

'Never trust a man who says he understands women!' she stated emphatically.

Trace managed a weak smile. 'On that count, I reckon I never met a man I didn't trust ... unless you count my pa. He might not have understood women, but he sure enough had a way with them.'

'I'm glad you didn't inherit the kind of charm he possessed.'

'Yeah, adultery is one of the worst sins in my book – the Good Book too.'

'And you don't commit any transgressions yourself?'

'I admit, I'm a few sins short of being perfect.'

She displayed a mischievous simper. 'Any sinful thoughts concerning me?'

'Desire comes to mind,' he confessed wryly. 'Reckon I'll do penance for that.'

'I guess that depends on whether your intentions are honorable or lustful.'

He arched his brows at her boldness. 'Uh, I'll go with whichever one doesn't get my face slapped or a dressing down from the parson.'

She laughed merrily at his answer, and it was a wonderfully musical mirth. '

Alter the conversation to a serious note, he asked: 'What is your father going to say about you dancing with me?'

'Oh, he told me not to even think about it.' She gave a puckish tilt of her head. 'So I didn't think about it -- I just did it.'

Trace stopped right in the middle of the floor, almost being run into by Lonnie and Tish. They hastily changed direction and Trace began dancing once more. He regarded the girl with a curious apprehension. 'Are you trying to start a war?'

Melanie shook her head, the long curled locks swaying from the gesture. Her eyes locked with his, showing a firm resoluteness. It was similar to when she had confronted him after the attack. This was a strong-willed, self-reliant girl.

'You saved my life, Trace McCain,' she declared softly. 'No man has ever done that before. I'll not pretend it didn't happen.'

'I told you how it was,' he said. 'I had already tracked those two Indians. I was going to kill them anyway.'

'Actually, I didn't ask you to dance because you saved my life. I asked you because I thought you liked me.'

Trace was shocked by her admission. 'That's a given, Miss Kendall. I haven't discovered one single thing about you that I don't like.'

'Then you may call me Melanie,' she said with a deliberate poise. 'I refuse to be called *Miss Kendall* by a man who saved my life, and who I happen to like.'

'You? Like me?'

His incredulity broke her serious mien. 'Is that so improbable?'

The music came to an end a moment later, but there was a great silence in the room instead of the normal conversation. Everyone was watching the figures of Lex Banning, Randy Kendall, and three other men. The five of them moved over to confront Tish and Lonnie, before they could exit the dancing area.

Trace immediately stepped over to stand next to Lonnie. He wasn't surprised that Melanie had the nerve to stand beside him.

'Let's not have any trouble,' Trace said easily. 'This is a community dance – let's keep it civil.'

'Won't be no trouble, McCain,' Lex growled, 'if this sleazy brother of yours takes his grimy paws off'n my sister and gets the hell out of here!'

'That goes double for you!' Randy directed his words at Trace. 'We don't want your kind around our women.'

'I'll dance with whomever I choose, Randolph Kendall!' Melanie shot back before Trace had a chance to answer. 'You two clowns have no reason to hate these men. They've never done one bad thing to anyone in the valley!'

'Melanie!' Harvey Kendall's voice boomed, as he strode across the room. 'Come over here this minute,' he threatened, 'or I'll take a horsewhip to you!'

'This is wrong, Father!' Melanie maintained, steadfastly remaining at Trace's side. 'This man saved my life! Is this your idea of gratitude?'

Harvey was as big as Lex, but only in height. He stood about even with Trace, his red eyes glaring hotly.

'We don't have anything to do with the McCains,' he bellowed, directing his words at Trace. 'Your whole family is no damn good!'

Trace showed no outward emotion, noticing from the corner of his eye that Charo and Bud were coming to join the group. Dean was also moving up from behind. The fight he wished to avoid was only about one word or swing away from taking place.

Chapter Three

Melanie quickly pushed forward, standing between Trace and her father. Her back was erect, shoulders squared with determination. With arms stiff at her sides, her small fists were balled in anger.

'Stop it!' she fumed. 'You have no right to talk this way, Father. Is this how a Kendall shows his gratitude – insulting the man who saved his daughter's life?'

'This is none of your affair, daughter,' the old man snarled.

'My life is my affair, Father!' she barked right back at him. 'Your hatred is beyond reason. Yes, you lost a brother, but these men lost their father. You're being pigheaded and – '

A resounding slap cut off Melanie's words. Harvey barely struck her before a fist exploded against the side of the man's jaw. He staggered back and would have fallen, if not for Lex catching him.

The altercation could have started a full-blown brawl, but the town parson yelled at the top of his lungs: 'No! Stop it!' And ran out in the middle of the two groups. He waved his arms and began pushing everyone back a step, defusing the situation before it erupted.

'I have put up with this feud long enough,' he said. 'The matter was dealt with and settled! One man killed another, and that man was hanged as punishment. Why do you insist on continuing to hate one another? We are all citizens in the same valley, we all pray to the same God.'

'We didn't come looking for trouble,' Dean spoke up for the McCain family. 'But we're through being ostracized like lepers. This is our home and our country too. If it takes a fight to be left alone and able to walk the streets without being attacked or vilified, then we will fight.'

'Fighting can't be the only answer to this conflict,' the parson said. 'There must be reasonable methods open to both sides to settle your differences.'

'I'm settling one of the differences right now,' Lonnie spoke up boldly. 'Tish and I would like you to marry us, Parson – soon as we can set a date.'

That brought murmurs from the crowd, but Lex only glowered at his sister with a barely controlled rage.

'You are officially announcing your engagement?' the parson clarified.

'As of right now,' Lonnie said.

Tish moved up to stand at his side. 'We'd be grateful if you'd perform the ceremony, Parson,' she confirmed the request. 'We were hoping for next month, so we can have our home ready before the winter season.'

'I would be delighted,' the clergyman said, smiling with relief that the fight had been averted. 'And I would hope your union helps to mend some of the broken fences that still remain between the townspeople and the McCains. Let us all look to a more harmonious existence in Rio Blanco.'

'If it's harmonious,' a gent remarked from the crowd of spectators, 'maybe they ought to take over the music-playing for these dances.'

The jest brought laughter from the crowd, breaking some of the tension that had built up from the confrontation.

'Let's break this up and finish the dance,' the pastor called out. 'We've still time for another tune or two.'

Rather than stick around and test fate, Trace and the other McCains left the barn in a group. Lonnie hung back with Tish, saying goodnight and promising to meet up with her in a day or two.

Trace was almost to his horse before he heard his name called. He turned to find Melanie had followed him outside. He took a step back towards her, meeting her in an open space between buggies and tethered animals.

'I'm sorry, Trace,' she said softly, looking up at him with dark, sultry eyes. 'My father – '

'Yes, I know,' he said. 'We didn't expect a warm reception, but we wanted to make a statement. We have been outcasts for nearly two years.' He heaved a sigh. 'Maybe time doesn't heal all wounds.'

'Father and Uncle Randolph were very close,' she excused his relentless hatred. 'They grew up together, went to the war together, and they started the ranch together – the loss has grieved him terribly.'

'I didn't intend to hit your father,' Trace admitted. 'It's just that … well, when he smacked you across the face … '

'Yes,' she murmured. 'I won't let him forget that, not for a long time.'

'No man should strike a woman.'

'It's the first time he's ever hit me,' she told him. 'That's what I'm trying to tell you – the loss of his brother is something he hasn't yet dealt with.'

'We could be just as bitter about the death of our father. He was a no-good skirt-chaser, but Randolph did have a gun. Both of them drew their weapons. Had places been reversed, Randolph would have gotten off without so much as a slap on the wrists. John McCain was hanged.'

'He attacked another man's wife,' she reminded Trace.

'Actually, the proper statement would be -- he *seduced* another man's wife,' he corrected her carefully.

She frowned. 'I was told – '

'Truth is, they were both cheating on their mates. Pa was no more guilty than your aunt.'

A glimmer of understanding entered her mien. 'That's why Father is so against you. Wasn't that brought out at the trial?

'Pa only had one decent bone in his body,' Trace admitted. 'He kept his mouth shut.'

'Well,' she dismissed the episode, 'I forgive you for hitting my father tonight.'

'And I thank you for standing up with us. I'm right pleased you have such courage.'

The corners of her mouth turned up slightly. 'I can't exactly return the compliment,' she fretted. 'I mean, you didn't even stick around long enough to tell me goodnight.'

'I was afraid it would cause you more trouble. I didn't – '

'After my standing up for you,' she pursued the argument, 'I believe I deserved something more, some tiny bit of consideration.'

'I'm sorry, but – '

'I'm beginning to think you McCains only worry about yourselves. Don't you care what I think?'

'Of course. But – '

'Then the very least you could do would be to offer me a smile and say a proper goodnight or something. Don't you – '

This time, it was Trace who cut her off in mid-sentence. He took her by the shoulders and pulled her into his arms. He kissed her – not passionately, or forcibly – but with a gentle coercion. Her lips were wonderfully receptive, much more than he expected. The intimate contact seemed to lift his feet off of the ground and a lightness filled his chest.

Then Melanie pressed her hands against his chest, and he immediately released her and stepped back. He held himself ready, in case she slapped his face. It would have been deserved, even though she obviously had not tried to prevent the kiss.

Melanie smiled up at him, an odd sort of simper, like nothing he had ever seen before. It was part seductress, part imp, and all woman.

'You struck me as a man of action, rather than words,' she teased.

'I didn't mean to … ' he began to apologize.

'No,' she interrupted. 'I shouldn't have let you – '

Thinking better of it, he prevented her from finishing, 'To tell the truth – right or wrong -- I've been wanting to do that since I first laid eyes on you.'

'Would that be the moment when that Indian had his fingers laced through my hair and a knife about to strike?' she asked. 'If so, I'm surprised you managed to hit him instead of me.'

He chuckled. 'Melanie Kendall, you have a most precocious wit.'

Her brows crested at his statement. 'Why, Trace McCain, you sound like a widely-read man. I would have never guessed it.'

'Ma had to do something at nights while Pa was off drinking, gambling and making a fool of himself. She liked to read aloud to us boys, and often explained the words or terms.'

'I believe I would like your mother,' the girl said. 'I've seen her at church meetings, but Father has forbid me to speak to anyone in your family.'

'He best never lay a hand on you again,' Trace warned. 'I'm not proud of punching a man twice my age, but I won't stand by while – '

Melanie placed two fingers over his lips to halt his flow of words. She then stepped back and touched the two fingers to her own lips.

'Goodnight, Trace,' she murmured.

He remained awestruck over what had taken place the past few moments, but he managed to raise his hand in farewell. He watched her as she returned to the barn, where the music blared into the serenity of the night.

'So that's Melanie Kendall,' Charo said cynically. 'Yep, homely as a sway-back cow. Your a swine, dear brother! And here she is, the picture of purity, beauty and innocence. You lowdown river rat, you wanted her all to yourself!'

'I didn't want any of you to get involved with a Kendall,' Trace told him. 'If I'd have said she was the prettiest gal in Texas, you'd have jumped on your horse and scooted right over to the Double K. Probably have gotten yourself shot, and I'd have been to blame.'

'If you're expecting thanks – forget it,' Charo griped. 'It's too bad she's already made her choice. I was sure she'd slap your face for kissing her. Durned if I know why she didn't!'

'Why don't you g'awn home,' Trace grated in a mocking tone of voice. 'Ma will be worried about her best-looking son.'

Charo chuckled, but, as he walked away, began to hum the Wedding March. Trace grabbed a handful of dirt and pebbles and tossed it at him. It only brought forth a laugh as he swung aboard his mount and headed down the road.

'What was that all about?' Lora asked, as her and Dean's buggy came alongside of where Trace was standing.

'Just cussing and discussing,' he evaded. 'You know Charo.'

'Oh,' she said with a smirk. 'Yes, I can certainly understand the cussing part.'

***

Trace found it hard to sleep. He arose shortly before sunup the next morning with red, tired eyes. He washed and shaved, and was sitting at the breakfast table when Lora and Ma McCain began to decorate the table for the morning meal.

'You feeling all right, son?' Ma asked, her owlish scrutiny never missing a thing.

'I'm wondering, Ma,' he spoke seriously to her, when Lora made a trip out to the fruit cellar to get some potatoes. 'Why did you marry a bum like Pa?'

She shrugged. 'He had a way about him … swept me off of my feet. I didn't know he would keep doing it to other women our entire married life.'

'He must have given some indication of his wandering eye.'

'By the time I realized he was a womanizer, Dean was a fact of life. You're pa was a good provider, and he kept me with child for the bunch of you. I always wanted a little girl, but it didn't happen. Now I have Lora … and pretty soon, Tish will be a part of our family too.'

'It doesn't change the rotten kind of man he was.'

His mother leaned over, showing a dead-set serious expression and spoke softly, so only he would hear her words. 'I didn't have a choice about marrying your father. He was always a handsome man, and he had such a way with words – by the time I knew his true nature, it was too late. You know what they say about babies?' At his frown, she continued. 'The first child can come at any time, but the others take nine months.'

As Trace wondered what she was going on about, he sought to clarify the meaning of that bit of uncomfortable wit.

'Dean was born the same year you were married,' he commented. 'But his birthday is mid-November, and your wedding anniversary is early January.'

'We altered the date back when we moved from Dallas. We had only been married a little over six months when Dean was born.'

Trace gulped ignominiously. 'Oh.'

'I confess this to you, Trace,' she was very sedate, 'because Lora mentioned you kissed the Kendall girl last night.' He started to speak up, but she held up a hand to stop him. 'I wanted to caution you because I know from experience that … well, sometimes things happen before they should. Don't make a mistake you will regret all your life.'

'Yes, ma'am,' Trace vowed. 'I was a mite impetuous last night, but I won't cross any other lines.'

She smiled. 'See? You're all grown up. We are able to converse on adult subjects.'

'I think I prefer to stick to teasing Charo or Bud,' Trace said uneasily.

'Well, you wanted to know *why* I married your father,' she reminded him. 'But I would prefer you don't tell the boys – especially Dean.'

'You got my word on that,' he promised.

'About you and Melanie ... ?' At his nod, she went on. 'Isn't it a rather dire and hopeless position, you wanting to court a Kendall?'

'I reckon Melanie figured she owed me for killing those two Apaches at the river,' Trace reasoned. 'She offered to dance with me, and ... well, I didn't intend to kiss her.'

'With Lonnie making his feelings known for Tish, and you making hay with Melanie – I'd say we've reached a point where the people of Rio Blanco are either going to have to accept us or run us out of the valley.'

'Yeah, Ma,' he agreed.

'Go out to the smokehouse and bring in a slab of bacon from the salt barrel, would you?'

'Right away,' he said, jumping up from the table. He made the trip out back, picked up the bacon and returned to find Charo was up. He was quick to grin at Trace.

'Bet you didn't get five minutes of sound sleep last night,' he sounded off like a crow in an unguarded cornfield. 'A guy's first kiss will do that!'

Ma frowned. 'Don't you go to teasing, Charo,' she scolded him. 'Trace is not a child anymore, and a wife wouldn't hurt him one bit.'

'Chasing after a Kendall girl could sure hurt him,' Charo argued.

'Randy or Harvey is bound to put a bullet in his gizzard!'

'Get the pancakes on the griddle,' Ma told Lora, ignoring his remark. 'Let's get these boys fed and off to work.'

'Yes, Ma,' Lora replied obediently. 'Dean is rousting the boys.'

Ma put her hand on Trace's shoulder. 'You're old enough to know your own mind, son. Don't you pay no never-mind to the others in this house.'

He patted her hand. 'I'll take it slow and easy, Ma. It's a tall mountain of hatred on that side of the river; gonna take a lot of work to climb over it.'

The meal was eaten with gusto and speed, as there was much to do. Dean was the foreman, in charge of daily work details. Once they finished cleaning their plates of the last bite of food. Charo left to milk their two cows, a chore he didn't mind in the mornings. He claimed milking was a good exercise for keeping his hands strong, which he needed when practicing with his gun.

'We'll divide the cattle into two main herds today,' Dean began. 'Once we get the main herd up the canyon, we'll haze the others to the lower pasture. That way we can get by with only two night riders, and they will be close enough to help one another, should trouble come calling.'

'Do you think those bandits would take on a ranch like ours without looking it over first?'

'We have to be on the lookout for every rider to come into the valley,' Dean said. 'That's why we put a sentry on Eagle Point.'

'What if they hit the town instead?' Lonnie asked, obviously worried about Tish. 'We didn't get around to setting up a warning system with them.'

'If we see them enter the valley, we'll gather what men we can and follow after them. If they try something, we'll be right close at hand.'

'Depends on how many men we're talking about,' Bud pointed out.

'What if there's fifty of them? Someone said they often have a bunch of renegade Indians riding with them. Against that many, we couldn't even defend the house.'

Charo entered the dining room with a bucket in his hand. 'Hey, anyone want some fresh milk? It's good for what ails you.'

'We were just discussing the duties for the day,' Dean informed him.

'Well, don't you boys worry about the bunkhouse,' Charo offered. 'I'll personally test every bunk and make certain they're comfortable. If you like, I'll even warm them up for you boys.'

'You're working with Benez, from the north rim to the basin,' Dean ordered. 'I'll work the big herd with Stoco and Bud, while Lonnie can relieve Francisco for sentry duty. He'll need the rest so he can stand watch again tonight.'

'You left me out,' Trace said. 'What's my job?'

'I want you to ride the river today,' Dean told him. 'Pick up any strays and haze them towards home. Either Bud or I will circle out that direction and pick them up. With the water so low, we probably have some of our cattle crossing over onto the Kendall land. No need causing any more trouble betwixt us than there is already.'

'I'll push any of their brand to their side of the river as I go,' Trace said. 'Wouldn't want Harvey claiming we were trying to steal his cattle.'

Dean gave a final nod. 'OK, everyone knows where everyone else will be – in case of trouble. Let's get to it.'

Chapter Four

Trace moved in a zigzag course, through thorns, cactus and low-hanging tree branches.

It was hot, dusty, thirsty work, looking for strays, and Trace found himself at the head of the river shortly after the sun was straight up above him. Deciding he and the horse needed a break, he rode over to the spot where he'd come to Melanie's rescue. Somewhere inside of him, he hoped that, by some mere chance or miracle, she would be there.

The water was cool and refreshing, and he let his horse drink after first cooling him down for several minutes. Then Trace put him in the tall grass near the shore and sat down with his meager lunch.

He had finished eating, and was refilling his canteen, when he heard approaching horses on the far side of the river. He took hold of the butt of his pistol, watching for whoever it was to come into the open.

A shadow moved through the trees, then a second, and a third. Trace pulled the gun and took cover behind a tall oak that stood near a log that bridged the water. He waited until he could clearly see the first rider was a Mexican. He remained concealed as a second Mexican appeared. They appeared harmless, but he maintained his position.

Finally, to his utter surprise and delight, Melanie Kendall appeared, chatting back and forth with the two men.

'Miss Kendall!' Trace called. 'What are you doing here?'

She spoke to the two men with her, and they both turned their horses back up the path through the trees. Then she climbed down from her mount, crossed the log adroitly, and jumped over next to Trace. He managed to get a hand on her arm and steady her landing, but he was completely perplexed by her arrival.

'Hi!' she greeted brightly. 'I thought it would be you.'

'Say what?'

'We've been riding the river below you, sending your cows across the river and turning ours towards home. Dad isn't taking any chances with those bandits or rustlers or whatever they are being close by. We are bunching the herd until something is done about the raiders. I managed to talk Pa into letting me help Ruban and his brother.'

'But you said you thought it was me. How did you know I was ahead of you?'

'From the number of cows we spotted heading for our place. Someone had to be driving them across the river from your side, and I – well, I assumed it would be you.'

'There are a half dozen of us working cattle today. I don't see how you could know it was me down here on the river.'

She laughed, her eyes sparkling. 'Maybe I was just hoping it was you.'

Suddenly Trace was struck by Charo's description of her.

'Purity, beauty and innocence,' he murmured.

Melanie blinked in surprise. 'What?'

'Uh, something me and Charo agree upon. I didn't mean to say it out loud.'

'As you were looking at me when you said it, I presume it was meant to be a compliment.'

Trace was lip-locked, unable to get his brain to function. *Give me a savage on the warpath;* he begged silently -- *a dozen gunmen aching for a shootout; an angry mother bear, or a rattlesnake in my bed ...*

anything but trying to woo a girl!

'Miss Melanie,' he confessed, 'I would be right proud to know the words to compliment you proper. I would compare you to the wonder of the stars above, or the serenity of a spring morning after a rain. But I haven't had any practice. You're the first girl I ever … wanted to impress.'

Her teeth flashed, as a glowing smile lit up her face. 'Thank you, Trace,' she said, without teasing or a hint of criticism. 'That is the most flattering compliment a man ever said to me.'

Trace was stunned by her response. He felt a warmth creep up his throat, a lump forming that made it difficult to swallow. In his mind's eye, he recalled the vision of her standing in the stream – wet, shivering, fearful … yet alluring, desirable --

'Uh, it isn't safe for you to be out here,' he said, trying mightily to suppress the vision. 'That gang could come along at any time, and there are still the Apache and Comanche to deal with.'

Melanie's smiled faded. 'We learned a little more about the raiders, after you left the dance. An ex-army scout was passing through town and stopped for the free punch and pastries. He told us the bandits are called Eller's marauders, and it is run by Dutch and Hutch Eller, a couple of brothers who have been raiding since the war. They have all manner of desperadoes in their group – any race or creed, all with a price on their heads. The law is unable to deal with them and the army doesn't have the manpower to patrol the entire border. The gang has done a lot of looting as well as rustling.'

'All the more reason you need to be careful. If your pa learns you've talked to me again, he'll take a strap to you.'

'No,' she said unwaveringly, 'he won't. We had quite a … discussion last night. I told him in no uncertain terms that I will never allow him to hit me again. He apologized, although he did a lot of hollering too, but Father knows I mean what I say. He won't lift a hand against me again.'

'You're a headstrong woman, once you make up your mind,' Trace pointed out. 'I wonder if you wouldn't be too much for a man to handle.'

A coy smile curled at the corners of her mouth. 'For the right man, I'd be everything he'd ever want in a woman. Until the other night, I never kissed a man after only meeting him twice and dancing with him once. I should be ashamed of allowing … ' she blushed noticeably and changed the wording, '...*encouraging* you to act so impulsively, but I'm not. I don't believe in teasing or toying with a man's affections. I don't want to lead you on unless you are truly interested in … in something more than a casual friendship.'

Trace took a deep breath, his heart pounding harder and louder in his chest than a dozen Indian war drums. 'Miss Melanie,' he said, his voice ringing inordinately husky, 'you turn my blood to fire. And I would be downright provoked if you were to say something like that to any other man besides me. I never dared dream a intelligent, wonderful girl like you would even look my way.'

Melanie moved over to sit on the edge of a fallen log. Trace followed after her, and sat down at her side.

'Do you have time to just talk?' she queried. 'I mean, for a few minutes?'

Trace decided the work could wait. 'It would be my pleasure. I'd sure like to know more about you.'

The girl laughed. 'If you want, I'll give you my life's story.' Then simpering, 'though it's a very dull, boring story indeed.'

Trace laughed too, though he didn't really know why. It just felt good – he felt good. Better than good … he'd never felt better in his life!

***

It was dusk when Trace entered the yard. He was whistling a bright tune and still riding high from the visit with Melanie. It had been a hard day's work, but it had passed by quickly. Even though he was tired, his spirits were alive. Plus, Melanie had promised to meet him the day after next, having to go to town tomorrow for the weekly ranch supplies.

He had never talked to any girl the way he had talked with her. She was interested in everything about him, his hopes, his dreams, his plans for the future and a family. Everything. Never had he dared imagine meeting a lady as special as her. Yet, she had agreed to be *his* girl!

Trace was happily brushing down his horse with a curry comb when footsteps approached. He looked over his shoulder to see Charo standing in the barn doorway.

'Darned if you don't sound like the happiest fellow in the crazy house. Maybe I should insist on working the river country next time.'

'Whatever makes you happy, Charo. I'm an easy man to get along with.'

'Yeah? Since when?'

'Since now. I'd even be willing to let you beat me at cards tonight.'

'But only if there's no money involved, right?' Charo cracked back.

Trace grinned. 'There's a limit to my generosity.'

Dean has scheduled a night watch,' Charo turned to business. 'I've got the midnight-to-four, so I've already eaten and am heading for the sack. You are supposed to relieve me, so don't be late.'

'I thought the hired hands were taking turns up on Eagle Point?'

'They can watch the valley entrance, but not the cattle. If the rustlers were to cross the stream, they could come from anywhere along the river.'

'So where are you going to be?'

'Riding guard along the south rim of the box canyon. It's an easy place to defend and it is only a short way to check on the cattle down in the pasture.'

'All right. I'll meet you at the canyon entrance at four,' Trace promised.

'Ma will wake you,' Charo informed him. 'She's already in bed, so you have to eat whatever scraps you can find. Lora is going to handle the cooking, so she is turning in early too.'

Trace groaned. 'That means I get the chore of cleaning up after all of you. I should have come in an hour earlier.'

'Scraping bowls and gnawing the little meat left on the bone of the roast we had ought to bring you down from those clouds you're floating on.'

Trace faked innocence. 'I don't know what you're talking about.'

Charo put a finger to Trace's left cheek. 'Unless you've taking to using a touch of rouge and missed your lips getting pretty, I'd say the Kendall gal dug her hooks into you a little deeper today.'

Trace recalled the hasty kiss on his cheek hours earlier, before Melanie hurried back to join the two Mexican riders. He had thought about a real kiss, but Ruban had appeared to warn her that Randy was coming towards the river.

He put his hand to his cheek and began to rub, while Charo snickered loudly, wandering off in the direction of the bunkhouse. Even as he studied his palm, he could see a faint trace of ruby-red coloring. He hadn't thought about how florid and healthy Melanie's appearance was, but now realized she had applied a tiny bit of makeup to accent her lips.

Trace ate a quick, cold meal, then cleaned the only bowl that had been left unwashed. His mother and Lora were both excellent housekeepers – they had to be with so many men in the family. He struggled to get to sleep and seemed to have barely nodded off when his mother was gently shaking his arm.

'It's three-thirty, son,' she whispered. 'Better get yourself up and go relieve Charo.'

'I'm awake,' he mumbled back, raising up onto his elbows. He looked at the figures still huddled in their blankets and sighed. Having himself a girl had taught him a lesson – daydreaming in no way compensated for actual slumber!

***

Charo met him at the point of entry to the valley floor. He had rolled a smoke, which he passed to Trace. Trace took a couple puffs and passed it back. He'd never actually enjoyed tobacco. He'd seen men who were as stuck on it as some others were on laudanum. He'd heard stories how a man, controlled by tobacco, would sell the clothes off his back for a chew or smoke. Any substance that could get its hooks into a person in such a way – he wanted none of! However, he occasionally would roll or share a smoke to be sociable.

'Quiet tonight,' Charo said, his voice breaking the stillness. 'Two or three head of deer went down to water an hour or so back. They might return the same way, as I was downwind and they didn't catch my scent. If it's light enough to see, you might look them over. We could use some venison, if there's a good-sized buck in the group.'

'I'll keep an eye out.'

'Bud had the shift before me,' Charo said. 'He thought he could make out a couple campfires off to the west shortly after dark. Since he didn't have any field glasses, he couldn't be sure. I rode up as far as the crest of the mountain, but I didn't see anything.'

'It could be the bandit gang,' Trace observed. 'They wouldn't want night fires to give them away, but they'd be likely to cook an evening meal.'

'It'll be something else for you to watch for come daylight.'

'I learned yesterday, the rustlers are a band of raiders run by a pair of brothers – Hutch and Dutch Eller. Seems we read about them in the newspaper some time back.'

'I remember,' Charo said. 'Over thirty men, including a few Indians. If they are coming to the valley, we're going to need all the warning we can get.'

'You don't fool me for a minute, Charo,' Trace grunted. 'You're just afraid you might miss out on the fight.'

Charo turned his horse for home. 'You could be right, Trace, but I'd like to think I'm showing a genuine concern for the other folks in the valley. Any fella able to sweep Melanie Kendall off of her feet must have some real charm. I wouldn't want anything to happen to them folks – no

1

way you'll ever get another gal to fall for you.'

'You're a real pal, Charo,' Trace said sarcastically.

'What are brothers for?'

'That question has been bothering me since I was little,' Trace admitted. 'I used to think the Lord created women to test men, to drive us crazy, but I'm not so sure anymore. Brothers seem to do the very same thing.'

'I can go home to bed and be insulted in my dreams by some lovely vision,' Charo said. 'I don't have to sit here in the dark, in the cold, in the middle of the night, and be insulted by a homely brute like you.'

'I'll see you later,' Trace said.

'Yeah,' Charo answered, starting his horse along the trail down from the ridge.

Trace listened to the sounds of his brother's horse picking its way down the trail. The moon was out, but it was a new moon offering only a minute glow to light the world below.

Trace staked out his horse, loosened its cinch, then took his rifle and walked casually along the edge of the canyon entrance. The rim was a hundred feet or so higher than the valley below, but it had limitations about how far a man could see. If Bud had actually spotted a couple campfires, it could have been the raiders. That was not a happy thought.

***

As was the case with most every farm or ranch, the Kendalls were early risers, eating at daylight, so they could get started on the day by the time the sun peeked over the horizon. It was especially true during the summer months – get as much work done as possible before the suffocating heat of the afternoons.

Melanie helped set the table in the dining room with the cook, Greta, who prepared meals for both the hired men and the Kendall family. This morning, Melanie felt drained of energy, unusually tired.

There had been a stirring in her, a restlessness she had never known before. After her conversation with Trace the previous afternoon, she had found it impossible to think rational thoughts, let alone get any sleep.

She sipped the cup of coffee Greta brought in, careful to avoid the old woman's sharp scrutiny. Though she was a quiet, non intrusive sort of woman, her expression often reflected her thoughts. She had been with the Kendall family since Melanie's mother died, and although she was hired help, she often got involved in whatever problems the family had. A widow, who had needed a job and a place to stay after her only son was killed during the war, she had found a home with the Kendall family.

Greta threw a questioning look at Melanie and shook her head.

'Men!' she breathed the word so it only reached Melanie's ears. 'Can't live with 'um, can't rid the world of 'um neither.'

Melanie was shocked at her comment, but offered her a weary smile. 'Yes, a true dilemma,' she replied.

As the woman continued her cooking chores, Melanie pondered what was wrong with her. She had no appetite, was often staring off into space aimlessly, and constantly pictured Trace McCain in her mind. It was ridiculous, having met him for the first time at the river. She had seen him on rare occasions, along with all of the McCains, during the past couple years – never close up enough to evaluate each man. Five brothers, all cut from the same cloth, but as different as five kinds of fruit. Each had his pros, each had his cons, whether it be size, looks or personalities. Dean was domesticated, a married man; Charo was carefree and reckless; Lonnie was still filling out, but had the courage to court Tish Banning; and Bud was the youngest, about to leave his teenage years behind, not yet a man, but not a boy anymore either. That left Trace.

A warmth climbed up her throat from the mere thought of him entering her mind again. She knew part of her infatuation was due to him showing up to save her life. He had given up a position of relative safety to come to her rescue. He had fought to save her life and killed the two savages who would have scalped and killed her. Such an act was bound to sway her thinking.

But what had possessed her to invite his kiss? She hardly knew him! It was more than impetuous, it was downright scandalous! Yet she couldn't help herself. She knew he would never take the first step in her direction without a push. So she had pushed. What else was there to do?

Melanie looked up from her cup of coffee as her father entered the room. A scowl was on his lined, weather-worn face. He still had a swelling on the side of his jaw from Trace's blow, and his lingering vexation was apparent in his expression.

'I just fired Ruban and his brother,' he said pointedly. 'They have you to thank for that.'

'What?' she cried. 'Are you crazy! Those raiders could hit us any day!'

'You've only yourself to blame,' he barked back at her. 'They let you spend half the day with that no good offspring of the vermin who murdered Randolph!'

'It was not more than an hour!' she flared back at him. 'And you can't hold them responsible! I made the stop when we were hazing the cattle back home. I did it – not them!'

'It's time you and everyone else on this ranch learned that I'm the boss!' His voice was harsh, his face red with his inner fury. 'I'm the boss and what I say goes!' he raged vehemently.

'I thought we had this out after the dance, Father!' she refused to back down. 'I am going to have some say in my life. You can either accept that or I'll leave home.'

'You'll do as I say, daughter!' he roared. 'If you don't stay away from that lowlife cutthroat, McCain, I'll kill him!'

Trying to regain a calm she didn't feel, Melanie rose to her feet. She didn't flinch from her father's burning eyes. She knew him well, and it was not wise to back away from him – ever. He was domineering and dogmatic, but the only thing he respected was strength.

'It's too late for you to intervene, Father,' she said steadfastly. 'I'm quite sure I've fallen in love with Trace McCain. He's strong, competent, a gentleman, and every bit a good man. If you weren't so dead set against the McCains because of Uncle Randolph, you would agree with me one hundred percent!'

The old man's mouth worked and his features twisted into a mask of disbelief. 'Love!' he said with distaste, curling his lips. 'You can't be in love with a man you've only been with for a few hours. Have you lost your mind?'

Melanie remained erect, defiant. 'What I've lost is my animosity towards a family for the actions of one man. And that man paid for his dastardly deed with his life.'

'John McCain attacked Randolph's wife – he killed my brother!'

She shook her head. 'John didn't attack Aunt May – she met him at the line shack. You have lied to me all this time, but I know the truth.'

'The truth!' he spat out the words. 'The truth is, the two of them were happy until John McCain come sniffing around like a dog, seeking to degrade any female he could get his hands on.'

'Yes, he was a vile cur, Father. But it was a seduction, not an attack. Both parties were guilty.'

Harvey's shoulders bowed under the weight of the truth. 'I'll admit, there was blame to go around, but it don't change the outcome. John McCain killed Randolph and shamed May for the rest of her life.'

'I'd say Aunt May shamed herself,' Melanie said quietly. 'And John paid for his deed.' When he had no response, she said: 'the McCains are our neighbors, our allies against the raiders if and when they strike.'

'I ain't runnin' to them begging help,' he grumbled bitterly. 'I'll die with a gun in my hand first.'

'And you'll let the marauders kill Randy too, then do with me as they please? Is that what you're telling me – that my safety, Randy's safety, and our entire ranch, means nothing to you? Is your hatred all you have to live for?'

He turned his back, as if he would leave the room, so she fought to try and reason with him.

'I'm your daughter, Father,' she said firmly, stopping him from walking away. 'I have many of your qualities. You should know by now you can't intimidate me with bluster or threats. Trust me when I say, you don't want to force me to choose between you and Trace McCain.'

The threat took some of the starch out of the elderly man. He hated the McCains, but he didn't want to lose his daughter.

'Don't do anything rash,' he said after a brief silence. 'You haven't been around McCain enough to know how you really feel. I'm sure your sudden affection is a result of him saving you from those two Indians.'

'I didn't go looking to fall in love with a man I knew you hated. And I've tried to separate the gratitude I feel from the wonderful way being with him makes me feel. You once told me that a person doesn't always choose who they love, sometimes love chooses them.'

The big man lowered his eyes, knowing a debate with his daughter was impossible to win. She knew his standards, his weaknesses, his loves. She could use his own convictions against him, along with her pouting looks, her somber eyes, and her blasted guileless beauty.

'We still need the supplies from town,' Greta broke the interim silence.

Harvey expelled a breath of resignation. 'Randy wants to ride in today,' he said to Melanie. 'So you don't have to go unless you want to.'

'I'd like to go,' she replied, knowing their bout was over. 'Martha Tibbs said they were expecting some bolts of material at the store. I could use a new blouse, and maybe even a dress for next month's dance.'

Harvey sighed in defeat. 'OK, yeah, buy whatever you need.'

Melanie offered him a warm, understanding smile. 'You turning generous on me?'

'It's the least I owe you,' he admitted, shame-faced. 'I can't believe

I actually struck you at the dance. I've never hit a woman before ... not ever.'

'I might have slapped you right back, but Trace pretty much evened the score.'

'Might be the son of no-good, philandering scum, but his punch is equal to being kicked by a mule.'

'He's also a very good shot,' she reminded him.

Greta stuck her head into the conversation again. 'If the war's over, I'll serve breakfast.'

'Thank you, Greta,' Harvey said. 'We're ready to eat.

Chapter Five

The dust rising in a small, far-off cloud was the first indication that a band of riders was headed for the valley below. Trace watched it for a while, moving his horse down the far side of the ridge, positioning himself in the rocks where he was concealed from view but able to see what was happening.

As he waited, he decided there wasn't ample dust to suggest more than a few horsemen, so it might not be Eller's Marauders. He reasoned it could be a small party of Indians, or even cow punchers seeking employment.

Trace removed his hat, squinting through an opening in the pile of outcropping rocks. As the men came around the end of the gully, he got his first look at them.

Eight men rode in a tight group, some white, some Mexican and one that could have been part or all Indian. They sported heavy Spanish riding saddles, the kind used by cowpokes, but with more silver and glittering conchos. Checking the mounts, the horses appeared to have covered a lot of ground -- their coats were laden with dust and alkali. As for weapons, they were all heavily armed, with ammo belts strapped across their chests. Some had guns on both hips and there wasn't an empty rifle scabbard among them.

Trace decided this was not the full contingent of men Dutch and Hutch had in their gang. Melanie had warned Eller had Indians with him and men equaling forty or more. If these riders were part of the Eller raiders, it was likely some kind of advance group.

The cluster of travelers seemed in no hurry, nor were they

especially wary of their surroundings. It was as if they weren't worried about being seen or attacked, which was odd for such a small number. The show of confidence could mean the rest of their band was close by.

Trace watched until they rode past him and out of sight. Then he got on his horse and headed to the ranch. Some of the men would still be there. If not, he would find Dean and tell him what he'd seen. Once he gave the alarm, he would follow the unknown men long enough to determine their intentions. If they were going to cause trouble, he needed to know if it was in Rio Blanco or if it concerned their own or Melanie's ranch.

Dean was in the yard, having just saddled his horse. His older brother looked up anxiously as Trace arrived, then tied up his mount and waited to hear Trace's report.

Dean listened and then rubbed his chin thoughtfully.

'You think these might be Eller's men, but only a what – an advance party of some kind?'

Trace shrugged. 'They were armed for war, but didn't seem in a hurry. Plus, they didn't have anyone scouting ahead of them. It's hard to say what they're up to. I figured to ride after them and see what mischief they had in mind.'

'No Indians with them?'

'One that looked Indian, but he was dressed like the others – all in regular range garb.'

'All right,' Dean decided. 'You check on where they're going and see what they're up to. Want any company? Old man Kendall fired two Mexican brothers this morning. They showed up an hour ago and I hired them both.'

'What's in that old fool's head?' Trace asked in an exasperated tone. 'Doesn't he know we might have a war coming?'

'I believe you met the two new men yesterday – down at the river.'

Trace slapped his brow. 'Ah, for the love of – ' He shook his head.

'They were only doing what Harvey's daughter asked them to do. He's going to get everyone on his place killed, all because he hates our guts.'

'He and Randolph were inseparable, Trace. Much like you and Charo. One of you can't get in or out of trouble without the other being involved. You notice Randolph's wife left as soon as the funeral was over, and you can bet she never got a civil word out of Harvey.'

'Or a dime either, I'll bet,' Trace said. 'She left with the clothes on her back and a stagecoach ticket in her hand. Good thing she had some relatives to return to.'

'At least she never had any kids of her own,' Dean remarked. 'Although it might have made a difference in her ... what's the word – fidelity?'

Trace dismissed the subject. 'I'll go after them alone – less chance they will spot me that way. If they aren't looking for trouble, I'll watch them leave town. If they are, I'll get word to the house.'

'Sounds good,' Dean approved. 'Sod won't make it back for a few days yet. We are pretty much on our own.'

* * *

Randy limped around the rear of the wagon, coming over to help Melanie down. He stopped before he reached the front wheel, his attention fixed on the eight riders entering town.

'Don't like the looks of them,' he said.

Melanie was poised to step down from the wagon. She paused in position as the band of men continued up the street. Though their saddles and clothes looked like wranglers or cow punchers, they were a rough-looking mix of white and Mexicans. Dirty, unshaven, and heavily armed -- enough to start a war. Even worse, they rode with a haughty arrogance, as if they owned the town.

'Eller's Marauders?' she asked Randy.

'Might be some of his men,' her brother guessed. 'The two Eller brothers are big, have red hair and beards – so it described them in the newsletter. Hand me the rifle from under the wagon seat. I'd better be ready – just in case.'

'We don't want to force them into doing something rash,' Melanie warned him. 'It would look like we are expecting trouble.'

'All right,' Randy yielded to her logic. 'We'll wait and see what they do.'

Melanie accepted his hand and climbed down from the wagon to the wooden walkway. She tried not to stare, but kept watching the ruffian's approach.

As if rehearsed a number of times, the group suddenly split up, four on the left side of the street and four on the right. A Mexican man moved to the center of the street, while a white man from the other half moved out to join him. They purposely stopped in front of the sheriff's office.

Grinning from ear to ear, the Mexican pulled out his handgun, held it up in the air, then fired it three times.

'Everybody come!' he yelled. 'Everybody come now!'

Barney Cod came stumbling out of his office, his shirt only half-tucked into his pants, his hair still mussed from sleeping late. Lyle and Martha Tibbs came out of their store and stood next to Melanie and her brother.

'What's going on?' Lyle asked Randy. 'What's all the shooting about?'

'I'm afraid we're about to find out,' Randy replied, starting to move along the walk to join Barney's side.

Melanie followed behind him, picking up Tish Banning and Doc Myer along the way. Most of the townspeople, curious about the shooting, gathered about, all wondering what was happening.

'Good people of Rio Blanco,' the Mexican greeted them with a phony, wide-toothed smile. 'I am Armando Orozco, and I greet you with a warm welcome from Dutch and Hutch Eller.'

That brought an unnatural silence from the crowd, all eyes trained on the Mexican. He relished the attention, nonchalantly hooking his leg over the pommel of his saddle. He took a moment to push his wide sombrero back from his forehead and surveyed the people with cruel, unrelenting eyes. His gaze rested on Meanie, and she cringed inwardly.

'What do you want?' Barney finally asked.

'You have heard of our leaders – the Eller brothers?' Armando queried.

'We've heard that you butchered and pillaged Little Bend a few weeks back,' Barney growled. 'You're a real brave bunch, taking on a few remaining men from the war and a lot of women and children.'

The Mexican glared at the sheriff.

'They were *muy stupido*, Mr Lawman,' he said thickly. 'You will not be so foolish, will you?'

'I asked what you wanted,' Barney repeated, showing a surprising amount of courage.

'It is very simple,' Armando said. 'We want you to give us anything and everything we wish. If you do this, no one will be hurt, and we will not destroy your fine town.'

'And if we refuse?' Randy challenged.

The spokesman's hard gaze settled on him. 'That would be most unfortunate … for you, for all of you. We have forty more men a few miles from here, enough to level this town and kill everyone in it.'

'We have law here,' Barney stated boldly. 'You can't just ride in here and – '

'We can do whatever we wish!' the Mexican cut him off. 'Did you not hear me, old gringo? We can pit fifty men against your pitiful handful of townspeople. Fifty!' He shook his head. 'We are giving you a chance to remain unharmed, a chance to recover from what few things we will take. What good are your possessions if you are dead?'

'And how do we survive?' Doc Myer wanted to know. 'Many of our people are barely getting by. The loss of what little we have will break this town and leave us with nothing.'

'We offer you your lives,' Armando reiterated. 'That is all you get. We too are poor, with many mouths to feed. We seek only enough to supply our needs for a few weeks, until we can find greener pastures at a bigger, more prosperous town.'

'You can drop your drawers and sit in a cholla patch!' Barney spat out the words. 'You thieving, murdering devils get nothing from us!'

A scowl spread across Armando's face. 'Does this man speak for you all?' he demanded to know. 'Do you all wish to die for your meager possessions?'

Several people exchanged nervous glaces, but no one spoke. It was a silent agreement and the Mexican representative knew it. He turned his burning eyes on the sheriff.

'You will be dragged behind my horse until you an unrecognizable hunk of flesh. The rest of your people will die under out charging horses!' he cried, his voice ending in a high screech.

Then looking over at Randy and Melanie. 'And you,' he pointed a warning finger at them, 'you – you gimpy gringo! I will break your good leg and run my horse over you a hundred times. Then we will gave a good time with the pretty girl.' He laughed, an insane chortle deep in his throat. 'Eller's Marauders will burn this town to the ground – and all of you will die.'

It looked for a moment as if all hell would break loose. Armando had returned to sitting the saddle with both feet in the stirrups, his hand on his gun. The other riders had taken up fighting positions with their rifles out and ready.

Some of the women were pulling their children off of the streets, while the others looked on in unspeakable terror. At that moment, Trace McCain entered town, riding casually, although his right hand rested on his gun butt. He rode up to the Mexican speaker and stopped a few feet away.

For Melanie, she felt a rush of relief flood her senses. Trace McCain was here. Everything was under control.

As calmly as he could, Trace took a moment to roll a cigarette, put a match to it, then take a single puff, blowing the cloud of smoke in the air. His right hand returned to a position close to his gun, while he looked around with a casual interest.

'Looks like quite a gathering here,' he said. 'Anything important going on?'

Before the Mexican could speak, the man who had sat silently next to him all this time, took charge.

'Would you be the man called Charo McCain?'

Trace looked the man over, noted the tied-down, very cared-for holster on his hip, and gazed into a pair of cold, calculating eyes. He recognized the mortal danger this man encompassed.

'Charo is my brother,' he replied. 'How do you happen to know about him?'

'I've heard he is pretty handy at putting out candles. I was wondering how he would fare going up against something a little harder to put out.'

Trace appraised him a second time. 'Meaning you?'

'I've taken a few men on face-to-face,' he said without bragging. 'I'm still here.'

'Maybe I've heard of you,' Trace said. 'There have been a few quick guns making names for themselves ever since the end of the war.'

'Vin Lacy,' the man answered. 'I took Larry 'The Flash' Dilts over at Fort Worth.'

'Seems I read about that – real standup, genuine, shootout, right on the main street,' Trace acknowledged.

'You tell your brother that I'm looking forward to meeting him,' Lacy said with a thin smile.

'Knowing Charo,' Trace riposted, 'I imagine he'll ride his horse to death just to make your acquaintance, Lacy.'

'We won't be hard to find,' the gunman said. 'We'll be back in a couple days, with a small army. Tell him not to get killed until we get a chance to meet.'

Trace turned deadly serious. 'Best stay to the rear of the pack, or else you'll be dead long before you reach the town. You don't want to test the mettle of the men of Rio Blanco. It'll be your end.'

Lacy continued his smug simper, tipping his head to the Mexican. As one, they turned about and started out of town. The other six men fell in behind them, none of them bothering to look back over their shoulders.

'We didn't need your help, McCain!' Barney snapped at Trace. 'You only made matters worse.'

'Worse than what?' Trace wanted to know. 'It looked to me like a gun battle was about to start.'

'Yeah, well, we were trying to talk them out of burning our town to the ground. You removed that option.'

'Those fellows were primed to kill everyone on the street,' Trace said. He took a moment to look around. 'I see three men with guns. Tell me, Barney, how exactly were you going to stop them from killing a bunch of women and children if a fight started?'

Barney threw a quick look around. Two or three of the men had taken their wives and children off of the street. Only he and the storekeeper were armed ... other than Randy. He licked his lips, knowing Trace was right. If the shooting had started, he and all opposition would be dead by now.

'You rode in as if you were declaring yourself in this fight,' Randy broke the uncomfortable silence. 'Is that your intention, McCain?'

Trace let out a slow breath, forcing himself to remain patient. 'We've been trying to convince everyone in this valley that we are a part of this town, this valley. One of these days, you and the others might understand we mean to stay.'

Barney softened his stance, wise enough to know he'd spouted off like a durn fool. 'McCain,' he invited, 'I'd appreciate it if you would join me, Doc and Lyle in my office. Randy, you best come too. We need to talk this over.'

Trace took a moment to tip his hat towards Melanie. He enjoyed the warmth that surged through him as she smiled. She was bold, defiant against the remaining hostility of the town, much the same as Tish Banning. She was no longer hiding her affection for him.

Inside the small jail, Barney sat behind the desk. It was the only chair in the room, with the lone cell providing the only other place to sit – bunk beds. Therefore, Randy, Doc, Lyle, and Trace remained standing in a circle facing the lawman.

'Any suggestions on what we should do now?' Barney asked.

'Depends on how long we have, don't it?' Lyle said.

'They rode in on worn-out horseflesh,' Trace pointed out. 'I spotted them at the upper end of our ranch, so they've come a great distance. Bud thought he saw their campfire back in the hills, so the remainder of the Eller gang must be at least a day behind them, maybe more.'

'How do you figure?' Barney wanted to know.

'If the main bunch had been within a few hours, those eight wouldn't have come into town on their own.'

'What purpose did they serve in showing their hand?' Doc asked.

'Two fold,' Trace answered back. 'First off, they were able to take a look at our numbers, so they would be aware of the opposition. And second, if you would have chosen to let them ransack the place, they might have simply done it and been gone.'

'Why should they think we'd give up without a fight?' Barney questioned Trace's logic.

'Because the news of Little Bend has gotten around. There are a few towns with even less fighting men than Rio Blanco. We have two ranches to add to the numbers here, but if we weren't involved in the fight, you would be easy meat.'

'So we've got two days or so,' Barney figured. 'That isn't much time to build a fighting force – not against upwards to fifty kill-crazy bandits.'

'How many men can we raise?' Doc queried.

Barney looked at Randy, who had remained silent. 'How many men can you provide?'

Randy uttered a sigh. 'I'm afraid it isn't that simple, Barney. What if they decide to hit one of the ranches first? We've bunched up the cattle where we can protect them, but we're short-handed as can be. Plus, Pa lost his temper and fired a couple of our hands last night.'

'We're looking at the same problem,' Trace joined in with Randy. 'We have our women and homes to think of too. We can't pull all of our men away without knowing what the Eller gang intends to do. They've rustled a great many cattle in the past. The town might be their second or even third target.'

'I hear what you boys are saying,' Barney complained. 'But, even if I raise every man who can shoulder a weapon, including our few farmers, we will only have eighteen or maybe twenty men. And some of those aren't worth shucks in a fight.'

'Let's face it,' Lyle said. 'Only the McCains are equipped to tangle with men like Eller's Marauders, and they couldn't handle forty men alone.' He threw his hands up in a exasperated gesture. 'And, speaking honestly, I don't see that their family owes us one blessed thing, not when you figure how they've been treated since John McCain was hanged.'

Barney rose to his feet, the palms of his hands flat on his desk, leaning forward to stare hard at Trace.

'What about it, McCain?' he asked. 'Can we count on any help from you or not?'

'I'll have to talk it over with the rest of the family. We need to know what the Ellers plan is before we can commit. If he hits our place, we'll have to be ready for him. On the other hand, if they head for town, we'll be late arriving. You'd still have to hold them off until we could get here to help.'

'Same goes for us,' Randy agreed. 'We don't have enough men to defend our place against a band the size of the Ellers. We could make them pay, but no way we could beat that many men.'

Barney lowered his head in defeat. 'Then we will have to make a stand with the few men we have in town. That's a worrisome outlook.'

'Practically hopeless,' Lyle concurred.

'We have to fight with what we can muster,' Doc said harshly. 'We can barricade both ends of town, put out sentries to keep watch, and keep our guns handy.'

'What about us?' Randy wanted to know. 'We're pretty vulnerable out there on our own.'

Barney grunted. 'I'm afraid you'll have to be on your own. We don't dare leave the town undefended.'

Trace and Randy left together, as they weren't going to be involved in the city's basic defense strategy. It was the first time the two of them had stood alongside each other since the McCain family moved in and purchased the deserted ranch. It had been owned by a father and two sons who all died in the war, so they were able to buy it for the taxes due. Four years later and it was a bigger ranch with more cattle than the Kendall place.

'Now I have an idea of how your family must have felt these past years,' Randy said to Trace. 'Having to face the hardships all alone.'

'We've a bigger family than you,' Trace replied. 'That has made it a little easier.'

'Yeah, I wish I had four brothers to share the load with sometimes. This bum leg causes me a lot of pain if I sit a horse for more than a couple hours.'

'Ought to have an army or big city surgeon take a look at it,' Trace said. 'I knew a feller who broke his leg and it mended wrong. Darned if the surgeon didn't re-break it so it could heal properly.'

Randy pulled a face. 'I can think of one word to fit right now – Ouch!'

'Yeah, my sentiments too … but it worked. After the doctor finished, the guy healed up, lost his limp and was as good as new.'

Melanie had been picking up a few items at Lyle's store. She came out with a flour sack of groceries, saw them on the street, and started to walk towards them. Trace stared at her, struck by her graceful way of walking … even with a bag in her arms.

'Yesterday, I'd have started a fight with you for looking at my sister that way,' Randy remarked.

Trace hastily put his attention elsewhere, a bit embarrassed at being been caught admiring the girl openly.

'Just so you know,' he recovered his aplomb. 'I'll be asking for your sister's hand one day soon.'

Randy chuckled. 'That ought to be a sight to see. Bet my pa puffs up enough to blow the buttons right off of his shirt.'

'I don't suppose you'll be on my side?'

'Depends on whether we all pull through the encounter with Eller's Marauders.'

'Yeah, there is that little detail to take care of first.'

Chapter Six

Dean, Charo, and Lonnie were all waiting for Trace. Bud was on his way in, leaving their five Mexican riders out to watch the cattle and be on lookout for more of the Eller band. Trace waited for the youngest McCain after dismounting from his horse.

'Coffee is on, Trace,' Dean called from the front porch. 'Come on in and tell us what you've learned.'

Trace and Bud went to the house together, and after getting cups of coffee, they all found comfortable spots around the sitting room. Then Trace outlined what had taken place with the raiders, what the townspeople were going to do, and how they needed help to defend the town.

'They've got a lot of nerve,' Dean spoke up first. 'Most of those people have harassed us, called us names, and wanted nothing to do with any of us since Pa was hanged. Now that there's trouble, they expect us to desert the ranch and go protect them and their valuables.'

'You say a man named Lacy wanted to test me with a gun?' Charo followed up on what Trace had said.

'Vin Lacy,' Trace clarified. 'He had heard about your trick in putting out those candles.'

'He look capable?'

Trace nodded. 'I'd think twice before I spit in his coffee. He had the confidence of a man who'd been in more than a few fights. He named some fellow he'd killed in a street gunfight over at Fort Worth – Larry *The Flash* Dilts.'

'Never heard of him.' Charo shrugged. 'I don't guess it matters much. If he comes looking for me, I'll have to face him.'

'What about the town?' Lonnie wanted to know. 'If we don't help them, they won't have a chance – not against forty or more gunmen.'

'And what if they decide to hit us first?' Dean shot at him. 'We can't leave our place unprotected, and we haven't got enough men to take on an army like that.'

'Well, we've got a better chance with this house than being exposed in Rio Blanco. I'm going to bring Tish out here – and I don't care how it looks to anyone in town!'

'What's your thinking on this, Trace?' Dean asked, knowing he had the best brain when it came to tactics and warfare. 'How do we manage to protect two places at once?'

'Three,' he corrected. 'Kendall is short the two brothers we hired. 'His place wouldn't stand against the eight men who were in town today, let alone several times that many.'

'I don't know,' Bud said, speaking for the first time. 'There's a couple people in town who have treated us decent, but the Kendalls have done their best to keep the hate going against us ever since the hanging. If we're going to try and help the town, I'm for it. But, as for the Kendalls ... ' he didn't finish.

'You're right, Bud,' Charo told him. 'Except Trace is carrying a torch for Melanie Kendall. We can't very well sit by and let his future bride stop a stray bullet.'

'Even Randy broke the ice today,' Trace said. 'It's only the old man who's still against us.'

Dean looked around at each of his brothers. 'So, we have to devise a plan to protect the town, protect ourselves, and somehow help the Kendall ranch if they get hit.' He uttered a cynical grunt. 'Shouldn't be a problem.'

Trace outlined an idea. 'We'll keep watch at the valley entrance for the Eller bunch. Once we spot them, we'll determine where they are going. If they turn towards one of the ranches, we'll sound the warning and put however many guns we can against them. If they head for town, we'll go in from behind and give them a surprise welcome.'

'And if they split into three forces?' Charo asked.

'Protect ourselves first,' Dean answered for the family. 'We can drive off a dozen men or so without much effort. Then we'll split up and try and help the others.'

Trace stood up. 'I'm going to ride over and speak to Kendall. Like I said, Randy is on our side about this fight, so we'll decide how best to help guard one another's backs.'

'Might point out to him that they are the most vulnerable,' Dean said. 'The Eller gang could avoid the main pass by navigating around to the southern part of their range. They could take them out first and take possession of their cattle, before they continue on to Rio Blanco.'

Trace nodded to his warning before going out the door. He would saddle a fresh horse, and then he would need Kendall to listen to reason. The first part would be easy, as the corral was full of well-rested mounts. As for the second, Trace tried to muster some spark of hope – getting Harvey Kendall to listen to him? He was a fool for even making the trip.

***

Melanie stood off to one side of the room. She had never felt a stronger kinship with her brother than she did at that moment. Randy was standing tall, facing his much larger father. He had held his ground under the first barrage of vehement curses and wild accusations, holding firm on his position.

'We need them, Pa,' Randy maintained. 'The Mexican ranchos across the border will not come to our aid, and the closest fort is almost a hundred miles away.'

'We've held this land against raiding bands of rustlers and a half-dozen different tribes of Indians. The Ellers aren't going to run us off or steal us blind.'

'And how do we stop them?' Randy cried, losing patience. 'You fired Ruban and Jose! They were two men who would have stood by us in a fight. Now we've got maybe six men who can put up any resistance at all. We can't stand against a big, powerful enemy like the Ellers.'

'What would you have me do?' Harvey asked. 'You want me to crawl over to the McCains on my hands and knees and beg for their help.' He snorted his contempt. 'You have as short a memory as your sister!'

'I have a good memory, Pa,' Randy bridled. 'I remember sitting on Uncle Randolph's knee and listening to his stories by the fire. I loved both him and Aunt May, but she made a mistake – it cost two men their lives. We didn't lose any more than the McCain boys. They lost their father and have had to live with the disgrace of his actions.'

'He's right, Father,' Melanie chose that moment to join in. 'We need to set aside our differences for the sake of our ranch ... and our survival. We need to work with the McCains to somehow defeat and drive off the raiders.'

The old man took a deep breath, faced with the reality of the situation. 'Who says the McCains can even help? I'd only heard about the one demonstration Charo put on in town. You claim Trace killed two Indians with a single shot apiece, but that could have been luck. Besides that, they have their own ranch to worry about. Why should they want to help us?'

'Melanie is one reason,' Randy answered quickly. 'Trace is hooked real good, Pa. He was mooning over her like a lovesick puppy in town.'

'Randy!' Melanie cried, shocked at the statement. 'Don't you be saying something like that!'

He grinned at her. 'And I noticed you were quick enough to return his calf-eyed stares.'

Melanie felt the heat of mortification. 'Y-you're jumping to conclusions, Randy. Yes, I admit that I like Trace McCain, but we've only shared each other's company for a couple hours.'

'I don't think Randy is exaggerating one bit!' Harvey took up against her. 'You've been giving me hell for bad-mouthing the man ever since the dance. I distinctly remember the word *love* entering into your tirade.'

Melanie swung her fiery gaze at one and then at the other. 'You men! You always stick together against me!'

'It's the only way a man can win a fight or argument with you,' her father said, allowing himself a wisp of a smile.

'Oh, yeah?' she fought back. 'Well, the only way we stand a chance against the Eller gang is with an organized effort from all of the men in the valley. We need the McCains to help us!'

Trace had ridden up unnoticed and walked onto the porch. He heard the last exchange and stepped into the room, uninvited.

'And the McCains could use your help too,' he announced.

All eyes turned on him. He held up his hands in a gesture of peace.

'The time has come, Kendall,' he began, 'for us to form an alliance. When Eller's Marauders return, they may intend to make a clean sweep of the entire valley – meaning us, meaning you, meaning everyone in town. We're going to need to work together to survive.'

'I don't like the way you've attached yourself to my daughter, McCain,' Harvey growled. 'And now you've got my son on your side.'

'There's only one side when you fight against a band like the Ellers – there's those who want to go on living, and those who allow their hate to destroy them and everyone they care about.'

'I suspect you are including me in the second half.'

Randy chose that moment to take his place between McCain and his father. 'Do you have a plan to defend the valley?' he asked.

Trace looked past him at his father. 'What do you say, Kendall? Can we call a truce for the time being?'

The man looked as if someone had let the air out of his sales. 'You've got both of my kids on your side,' he said in dejected voice.

'Guess I don't have any other options.'

'We know the Eller bunch will come from the south,' Trace outlined. 'We've put a sentry down that way to signal us when they approach. There's a chance, though, that they might turn at the river and come this way.'

'I've considered that, McCain,' Harvey informed him. 'I'm also putting a couple men at the far corner of our place to keep watch.'

'Eller probably knows our two ranches have the most able men in the valley. He'll want to keep us from uniting with the men in town.'

'I reckon that's true.'

'So if they turn your way, send word at once, and we'll come running with as many men as we can gather.'

'And I suppose the reverse is true,' Harvey concluded. 'If they hit you, we send as many men as we can.'

'That's right. Our biggest worry is if they split their forces to get rid of both ranches at the same time. If that happens, it's important to know how many men we are up against,' Trace continued. 'If you get hit by fifteen or more men, you'll be in real trouble. For us, we can handle a few more than that, because our house is built like a fortress and we have more men.'

'And if they head for town?' Randy asked.

'We join forces and hit them from behind. The people are going to put up a barricade, so they should be able to hold them off for a few minutes. If we catch them by surprise, we can do a lot of damage.'

Harvey thought for a moment. When he spoke his voice had lost most of its hostility.

'Even with all of us in the fight, it don't look good. We only have a few fighting men, and the town won't muster more than a dozen or so. We're going to be heavily outnumbered.

'If they turn on our ranch,' Randy warned, 'we won't last but a few minutes. We only have six or seven guns – not nearly enough to oppose a band of thirty or more men.'

'You could abandon the ranch,' Trace offered an option. 'Run the cattle back into the hills as best you can and ride into town to help from there. They might burn down this house and steal some of the cattle, but there's a chance to survive and rebuild.'

The old man shook his head.' Melanie and Randy were born on this ranch. We'll put out sentries and do what we can to coordinate with you concerning the town or your ranch. If Eller comes, we'll try and give his gang enough hell that he won't soon come back!'

Trace chuckled. 'I'm for that, Kendall, I surely am. We'll be keeping in touch.'

'Watch out for yourself,' Randy told him.

'The same goes for you people. We've more guns to defend our place – you'll have to react instantly, with such a small fighting force.'

'We'll react all right,' Harvey assured him. 'You call us, we'll come a-running. If we need your help – '

'We'll also come a-running,' Trace finished.

Then he left the house and mounted his horse. He looked back in time to catch a timid wave from the doorway. He smiled, returning the farewell to Melanie. She would be all the incentive he needed to come as quick as possible in case of an attack.

Even as Trace rode out of the yard, a foreboding settled on his shoulders. There was a time to daydream and a time to be realistic. He feared that, realistically, the chance of the McCains and the Kendalls coming out of the upcoming trouble unscathed was mighty slender.

***

The remainder of that day went to preparing an adequate defense around the house and outbuildings. Lonnie went into town and returned that evening with Tish, but otherwise there was no communication with anyone outside of those on the ranch. Pickets were set up, relief schedules and warning signals worked out. If the Ellers returned to Rio Blanco by the river canyon, they would know quick enough.

Trace took an early shift and was the first one up the next morning. He put on coffee before Ma was even rousted from her night's slumber. An hour past daylight, and after a limited family breakfast, Bud arrived from his stakeout. He had been on the Eagle Point, not far from where Trace had spotted the bandits the first time. His eyes were red from lack of sleep, but he stopped to have a bite to eat before taking a morning nap.

'Saw something strange this morning,' he told Trace.

'What?'

'It was just past daylight, so I was keeping a watch both up and down the valley – you know, in case those raiders sneaked by in the darkness. Well, anyway, I was sitting real quiet, gun on my lap, my horse tucked down out of sight. Then a lone rider appeared heading away from town. You'll never guess who it was?'

'I'm not in the mood to guess,' Trace said wearily. 'Spill it!'

Bud shook his head, as if in disbelief. 'It was Lex Banning, riding away from Rio Blanco as cool as you please.'

'Lex Banning? Wonder where he was going?'

Bud shrugged. 'I don't know, but the strange thing ... it didn't look like he was carrying a gun.'

'Ah,' Trace said, 'he had to be packing iron.'

'He's right handed, but I saw no gunbelt and no rifle sheath. I used the field glasses and checked to make certain. I'm telling you, Trace, he was unarmed.'

'It makes no sense. Unless the town got together and are willing to negotiate a deal of some kind with the Ellers – maybe the town's spokesman?'

'This is Lex we're talking about,' Bud replied. 'I think we have to look at the other possibility ... what if he's selling out the valley?'

Trace hated to even think along those lines. 'I don't see him doing that. Tish is – '

'Staying here with us,' Bud reminded Trace. 'She would be out of harms way.'

'Lex was real bent over Tish and Lonnie announcing their relationship,' Trace allowed. 'I suppose he could be angry or humiliated enough to turn against the town.'

'What'll we do?' Bud asked.

'I'll have one of the boys ride into town and inform Barney that Lex was seen leaving the valley unarmed. That way, they can deal with the information any way they deem necessary. If he happened to volunteer to ride to the bandit camp and make a deal to save the town ... ' But Trace knew Lex was not the type to volunteer for something like that. No, this had a very bad smell about it.

**

The Eller brothers were sitting near the camp's large fire with Armando when Lex Banning was led into camp. Smoke and the aroma of freshly roasted meat hung in the air from the butchered calf the men had eaten with their beans for supper. All small chatter and milling about came to an abrupt halt at the sight of the uninvited guest.

Hutch stood up first, followed by the other two. He and Dutch were both unusually big men, taller than most and built like beer barrels. Hutch used a hand to remove a lock of his long red hair from dangling into his eyes, the mane dark and greasy from weeks without washing. His fuzzy, unkempt face broke into a wide grin.

'Who have you brought us, Vin?'

Vin Lacy prodded Lex forward with the barrel of his rifle. The visitor reeked of hard liquor and the red in his eyes revealed a fair level of intoxication. 'This hombre says his name is Lex Banning and he wants words with you. He was unarmed and claims to have ridden all day to get here.'

Hutch noted the man's dire apprehension, the nervous trembling, the man's sweat-encrusted brow. The consumption of alcohol was not enough to prevent the fear from showing in his demeanor.

'Are you one of the Ellers?' Lex asked, his voice fairly quaking.

'I am Hutch Eller,' he replied. 'What is it you wish to say?'

'I'm from Rio Blanco,' Lex told him. 'I've come to make a deal with you.'

'Is that so?'

'Yes. I can give you useful information, information that will save the lives of many of your men.'

Hutch looked around at his men. They were all eying the stranger with open suspicion. He mustered forth another crooked smile. 'Tell me what you know that is so important to the lives of me and my men … and maybe we can do business together.'

Lex's eyes darted around, obviously realizing what a dumb notion this had been. He struggled to recoup the false courage the bottle of hard liquor rendered, but the true nature of how dangerous this was had begun to penetrated the inebriated fog.

'I want a man named McCain killed,' he began. 'And I want my sister to be left alone.'

Hutch considered his request, then looked at Vin. 'This is the name of the man you spoke of, is it not?'

'Which McCain you talkin' about,' Vin asked Lex, 'Trace or Charo?'

Lex gave a negative response. 'The one I'm interested in is Lonnie McCain. He took my sister out of town and is holding her captive at the McCain ranch.'

'Captive you say?' Hutch pondered. 'So how many McCains are there?'

'Five boys – one has a wife, and they have a couple of hired hands too. It's the Circle M ranch, on the east side of the river.'

'A ranch you say?' Dutch was the one to speak up. 'Would that be a cattle ranch?'

'Yeah, that's right. There's only two in the valley, Circle M on the east side of the river and the Double K on the west side.'

'It is a long way to drive cattle from here,' Hutch told Lex. 'We didn't intend to hit the ranches, only the town.'

'They'll catch you between them if you try to attack the town,' Lex warned. 'The ranchers will hit you from behind. They've worked out some kind of system to stop you.'

'So we have to first hit the two ranches. Is this what you are saying?'

'It's the only way,' Lex said, hurrying on to convince them of his worth. 'I can tell you where to ride in, how to trap the men on the two ranches, the way to keep from losing a lot of your men. You deal with me, and I'll steer you straight.'

Hutch allowed himself another smile, but it was more sinister this time. 'Tell us what you know, Banning. I'm sure we can make a deal.'

Lex began talking, pointing out the approximate number of men at each ranch, the probable location of their defense, and the weaknesses that could be exploited. Then he went to great lengths to explain the town's vulnerability.

Hutch and Dutch listened attentively, absorbing the information Lex outlined. For himself, Lex wanted to ransack the general store and then take his sister and leave the country. His deceit and treachery was so great, Hutch wondered why the man hadn't asked to join their gang.

When the traitor from Rio Blanco finished speaking, Hutch discussed the matter with his brother. Finally, his gaze flicked over to Armando.

'Do you think this man is telling us the truth, Armando?'

'I think he is not a man to trust. What if he is trying to split our forces by attacking the the two ranch strongholds? What if it is a trap?'

'No!' Lex cried. 'I'm not here to trick you. I told you why I came – I want my sister back, and I want McCain dead. If I can snag a little traveling money, that's all I'm looking for!'

'I think we should check his story,' Vin spoke up, not hiding his distaste over such treasonous behavior. 'Perhaps Cuerdo can get the truth out of him.'

Hutch emitted an evil chortle. 'You are right, Vin. Cuerdo has a lot of experience – him being a full Apache.' Glancing at Lex, 'he will learn the complete truth.'

'Wait a minute!' Lex cried. 'I'm telling you the truth! I came here to help you!'

Hutch bobbed his head at a couple of men and they quickly tied Lex to a nearby tree. Cuerdo came forward and selected a medium-sized branch that had been burning in the campfire. The one end had not yet caught fire, so he held it like a torch, walking over to where Lex was squirming against the ropes that held him.

Cuerdo shook out the flames on burning branch – he didn't need that much fire. Just enough heat to get the information he wanted. If Lex knew nothing, he would learn that too … although it was a foregone conclusion: the traitor from Rio Blanco would not survive the interrogation.

Chapter Seven

Trace was in the saddle at first light, riding the river once more. Charo was up at the canon rim keeping watch for the Eller gang. Bud and Lonnie were back at the house getting some well-earned sleep, and Dean and the rest of the men were moving the herd from one pasture to another. They couldn't let the cattle graze the ground bare or go hungry. If Eller came after the herd, he would be getting well-fed beef.

Riding the saddle of the ridge that followed the river for almost a mile, Trace was in a high enough position to see the canyon rim. He could also see across the river's foliage to the Double K side. There was no sign of movement, as the ranch itself was well out of view, but Trace sat in contemplation all the same.

Somewhere, a couple miles away, was the girl he intended to marry. The thought of the Kendalls being attacked by a bunch of the Eller men disturbed him deeply. They simply didn't have the manpower to withstand any kind of onslaught. With so few men, they would be overrun if even a handful of the marauders hit the ranch.

Trace was supposed to patrol the river and keep watch, but he decided this was as good a place as any to see both sides of the river. He found an egg-shaped boulder, propped his rifle against the rock and took a position atop it, sitting cross-legged.

Removing a piece of jerky from his shirt pocket, he bit off a portion and began to chew. Knowing he wouldn't be home until dark, a bountiful breakfast and a handful of jerky would get him by. The word from town was that Lex had been arguing with Barney and Lyle, extremely upset that Tish had left to join Lonnie at the McCain ranch. He had been drinking heavily and disappeared the next morning, telling no one where he was going. He had left his guns behind and taken only a bottle of whiskey with him. Nothing about his desertion sounded good.

As for the townspeople, there was no way to change their defenses. They only had so many guns to man the barricade, a few women to shoot from the top of the saloon – the only two-story building in town – and had already done what they could to wall up between the buildings. Their fear was the outlaw band would be able to circumvent their line of defense and sneak in via the alleyways.

The two ranches had not informed anyone in town as to their disposition or plan to ward off an attack, so Lex could not have told the Ellers much of anything but their approximate numbers. That made the Kendall ranch the easiest victim, but Lex would have wanted revenge. He would have tired to get them to attack the McCain ranch instead. At least, that was what Trace hoped. His family had a much better chance of fighting off the raiders than the Kendalls.

***

Melanie packed the roast-beef sandwiches into the burlap sack. She wished she had some fruit or something to go with it, but the men on guard would have to get by with what they had on hand.

'You about ready?' Harvey asked from the next room.

'Yes,' she answered, turning towards the room. She entered and stopped a step away from her father. 'Do you have any message to pass to Tom and Dale?'

Harvey frowned in thought. 'Only to keep their eyes open. Me and Shorty will be along about sundown to relieve them.'

'I'll let them know.'

'And, Melanie?' He hesitated as she looked at him. 'You keep a sharp eye out there too, you hear?'

She smiled. 'Certainly, Father. I won't take any chances if I see any riders coming.'

'We'll be working on barricading the house, so you will find us right here if there's trouble.'

'OK.'

He displayed a sly grin. 'And no wandering down to the river to see if your man is there – understand?'

'You don't trust me?'

He shook his head. 'It's McCain I don't trust. Trace is looking to steal you right away from me.'

She laughed at his serious tone of voice. 'Trace wouldn't have to steal me, Father. I'd go willingly.'

'Now I feel a whole lot better,' he grumbled.

'Better than if you had managed to get me and that ape, Lex Banning, together. I can't believe you preferred him as a suitor over Trace.'

He displayed a sheepish look. 'Yeah, I admit, I was getting pretty desperate. Lex ain't worth his weight in sand. If it wasn't for the money his pa left him, he would be a penniless bum. Tish is the only thing that family ever had worth her salt – and she's throwed in with a McCain too!'

'See?' Melanie teased. 'We girls have better taste in men than you. That shouldn't come as a surprise. Mom always said you were a poor judge of character.'

'She still married me,' he pointed out.

'Yes, because your judgment and temper were about the only flaws you have.'

He grunted an end to their joshing back and forth. 'Best get going or Tom and Dale will be thinking we forgot them. And,' he added again, 'be careful.'

'I will, Father,' she assured him.

Randy had her horse saddled, and he also warned her about keeping a watchful eye out for riders. It was near mid morning by the time she got her horse underway.

Melanie stayed out in the open, moving at a brisk pace. At another time she might have complained to herself about the sun's burning rays, the stifling dust from her horse's hooves, or the dryness of the air, but those things were not important on this ride.

She felt uneasy riding alone, and every sound, chirping of bird or chipmunk put her nerves on edge. There had always been the danger of Indians, for as long as she could remember, but this was different. She had regarded the Indians as part of the hostile land, something as natural as the other wild animals.

She had grown used to watching for them, avoiding the outer regions of their territory where she might encounter a roving brave or two. Now, with the threat of having her home and life utterly destroyed by a gang of killers and thieves, she could think only of them.

She had ridden the length of the valley when she stopped suddenly. There had been distant pops – the sound of guns being fired.

Melanie jerked on the reins of her horse, spinning him violently around. She heard more shots, as she spotted a group of riders coming over the far rise – Tom and Dale had been attacked and either ran for their lives or were already victims!

Digging her heels into her horse, she spurred him back towards the ranch. She cast a fearful glance over her shoulder and was able to see a stream of twenty or more men coming over the hill. They were a quarter of a mile away, but they had seen her. She was glad Randy had saddled Blue Boy, for he was one of the best animals on the ranch. With her head start, the bandits would never overtake her.

The horse was game, racing through the brush, following the vague trail, taking the long strides of a distance-running horse, eating up the ground effortlessly. He nearly unseated Melanie when he took a wide ditch with a long leap, jarring her teeth as he hit the opposite bank.

Randy shouted the alarm, seeing her coming towards the house. He father, Shorty and two Mexican hands were all there as she rode in.

'They're coming!' she shouted the warning. 'They overran Tom and Dale before I reached them. There was a lot of shooting!'

'Stay on that horse!' her father commanded. 'Turn Blue Boy for the McCain ranch. Get them over here – pronto!'

'We'll hold them off!' Randy added his assurance.

With a jerk of the reins, her powerful horse raced off down the hill towards the river. She kept him running full out. If she didn't get help – and get it fast – there would be no ranch to come back to!

***

Trace was on his horse, having heard the distant reports of gunfire. He searched with his field glasses, trying to locate either the battle or the riders. The shooting stopped as quickly as it started, the echo dying out before he could figure out where the shots had come from. He didn't think it was from Charo's position, and there had been no warning signal. He had to find –

He picked up the rider in his glasses, headed for the river crossing below. The figure was a long way off, but it looked like Melanie. At nearly the same time, he saw the warning puffs of smoke from Charo's position.

Trace was torn – what to do? He knew someone would be watching for Charo's signal from the ranch. They would be ringing the warning bell and preparing for an attack. As for Melanie, she had to be coming to get help. That meant her ranch was also under attack.

Lex Banning! Trace cursed the man under his breath. He must have informed the raiders about the two ranches. They had split their force to reduce both places to ashes before they hit the town.

Knowing his family had the better chance of defending themselves, Trace rode down from his lookout point to intercept Melanie. He saw her break from the shelter of the trees and raced to cut her off.

Melanie spotted him and reined in her horse. She was flushed from the ride, and fear showed naked on her face. She had to inhale a gulp of air before she could formulate any words.

'Coming!' she gasped. 'They're coming!' She took another breath. 'I think Tom and Dale are dead and they are headed for our house.'

'How many did you see?' he asked her, still torn between his loyalty to his family and his wish to help save her kin.

'Twenty or more! They must have guessed where our men were camped. I heard shooting and then they appeared. I barely had time to warn the house. If we don't get help, they'll kill Randy and Father!'

Trace hesitated. 'Charo just sent up the signal,' he told her. 'They're going to hit our place too. They have split their force to take us both out at the same time.' He shook his head. 'It would take too long to get any help from town … even if they would risk sending men to fight.'

'B-but … what'll we do? My father, brother — there's only five of them at the house. They won't have a chance!'

Trace knew his family, and their fortress of a house would withstand a lot more than the flimsy-built Kendall ranch house. They would be short only his gun, but Kendall had released his other two men — who would now be helping the McCains in their defense.

'Let's go,' he told her, making his decision. 'If we come in from the wooded ridge, we can help to even the odds.'

'Just you and me?' she asked, totally aghast. 'Trace, I've only shot a gun a time or two in my entire life!'

'You can reload for me,' he said.

She followed his lead as he rode back down and crossed the river. They cut across some open ground and took to the forested range that was on the ranch's northern front side. As they worked their horses feverishly through the maze of trees and tangled brush, the gunshots rang out from the nearby ranch. They were under heavy attack.

For the love of the girl who was right behind him, Trace knew he had to do whatever he could to help save her loved ones and her ranch. He headed for the small cedar-covered hill that was poised in a position to overlook the ranch and yard. By circling to the far ridge, he hoped he would be above the attackers. He needed the high ground to have any chance of both helping the people trapped below and preventing the raiders from getting at him and Melanie.

Reaching the crest, he stopped the horses, dismounted and grabbed his extra cartridges for his rifle. He handed Melanie the ammo as she tied off her horse.

She was winded, but looked anxiously at him. 'What now?'

'You stay low and behind me. The shooting is dying down, so I hope we're not too late.'

Trace crept over the rim and hurried down to a well-protected spot between two cedars and a few sizable boulders. He directed Melanie where to sit, so she would be able to reload his rifle if necessary and not be a target. When he peered over the rocks at the ranch below, he felt a sinking sensation in his chest.

There were bodies of three bandits in the yard, but there were fifteen or more men surrounding the house. They had shot out every window and knocked down the front door. Only a shot or two came from inside. Evidently, the only men left were fighting gallantly for their lives.

Trace raised his rifle, aligned his sights, allowed for the downhill slant, and squeezed the trigger.

A man threw his arms up, staggered out from behind his cover, and pitched forward on his face. His unexpected death turned a couple heads, wondering where the shot came from. It allowed Trace time to knock over a second man … and quickly, a third.

Several turned to shoot at him, but they were using handguns for the close assault on the house. He downed a forth before they realized he was out of pistol range.

One of the men waved his arms and shouted to the others. Trace rose up in time to make out the Mexican who had been the spokesman in town … Armando.

With every ounce of concentration he could muster, Trace followed the man's movements, waiting for an open shot. The man bolted for where they had secured their horses. He and the remaining men were all getting mounted. He got aboard his animal and paused to look up at Trace's position.

The look was his last. Trace pulled the trigger and Armando folded like a napkin, hunched over the horse's neck.

The men milled about in confusion for a moment, suddenly leaderless. Then one took the reins of Armando's horse and they all swung about and raced down the trail, heading back the way they had come. The direction was not towards town or the McCain ranch, so it was likely they were rejoining the rest of the gang.

'Cut off the snake's head,' Trace told Melanie. 'They're riding away – likely to a meeting place or their campsite.'

Melanie was on her feet. 'Let's get down to the house!'

Trace took the ammo from her and they got their horses. As they rode down the hill, Trace kept watch over any of the raiders who might still be alive. He didn't want to risk a bullet in the back by being careless.

'I'll check the bodies,' he told Melanie. 'You make sure whoever is still alive doesn't shoot you.'

'Go help your family,' Melanie said. 'I'll bring everyone that can ride to your ranch.'

'Good thinking,' Trace agreed. 'Ma is a passable doctor and twenty men isn't near enough of an army to overrun the McCain house. I'll ride over and see if I can do some damage like we did here.''

'I'll get everyone over there as soon as I can.'

Trace looked over the bandits, but anyone who was wounded had been helped to their horse. Melanie called out from the house: 'Go, Trace! We'll be along!'

Once more crossing the river, Trace concerned himself only with the direction from which he should approach the McCain ranch. He would have to be cautious, as riding into the middle of Eller's men could get him killed real quick.

The shooting was still distant, but it was steady. The attacking force had not caught the McCain's sleeping. They would pay for any damage they did. As for Trace, he hoped his luck would hold one more time.

Chapter Eight

Melanie had called out before going into the house. She stifled a cry, seeing Shorty lying on his face near the door. She recognized one of the Mexican hands near the window. Looking around the dark interior, the place was a shambles, covered with over-turned chairs, broken glass and several bodies. The smell of gunpowder and blood assailed her nostrils and burned her eyes. In one corner she could see the turned-over couch and a pair of legs.

'F-Father?' she said, tears streaking her cheeks. 'Randy?'

Someone moved, and she jumped at the sound. She located a shadow in the far corner of the room, a few feet from the couch.

'Sis?' Randy's strained voice ended the interminable silence.

Melanie hurried across the room and dropped to her knees next to her brother. She could see he was hurt. One arm was bloody, and he was pale – even in the subdued light.

'Trace got several of them,' she said quickly, tearing his sleeve to reveal his wound. 'He hit the one who did all the talking in town and they ran.'

Randy was seated against the wall, his eyes shut against the pain and exhaustion. He rolled his head from side to side, a sorrowful expression twisting his features.

'That's Pa, over behind the couch. I don't think he even knew he'd been hit.'

Melanie bit her lower lip, but her fingers continued to work. She stopped long enough to round up some disinfectant and clean cloth for a bandage. 'It looks like the bullet passed through, so we don't have to remove the bullet.'

'Is everyone else … dead?' she asked.

Randy opened his eyes, but they were misty, unseeing. 'Paco crawled into the bedroom, but he was hit hard. Greta was killed while reloading a gun for Pa. We didn't' stand a chance against so many guns.'

Melanie went quickly to check on the others, then covered her father with a blanket, and returned to her brother.

'If – if Trace hadn't driven them off … ' She let the words hang, knowing Randy was aware the man had saved his life.

'Where is he?'

'The bandits split up. Trace was across the river when I found him. His family had already signaled the warning for an attack over there. He came to help us first and has gone to see if they need his help now.'

'Give me a hand up,' Randy said, getting his good leg tucked underneath his body.

Melanie helped him up, then supported him as far as the door. He leaned against the frame and looked out over the yard. The bodies were sprawled around akin to a major battlefield scene.

'Damn,' he said softly.

'I agree,' Melanie whimpered, suffering from the shock of her father's death, along with all of their hired help. Everyone was dead but the two of them.

'Can you saddle another horse?' Randy asked. 'I think I can ride, but I feel too drained to lift a saddle.'

'I'll get one from the corral. The bandits left too quickly to take the livestock with them. We can either head for town or the McCain place.'

'The McCains,' Randy told her. 'It seems we both owe Trace our lives.'

***

Trace heard only sporadic gunfire as he approached, and before he could reach the ranch house, the shooting had stopped altogether. He caught a glimpse of several riders moving quickly down the southern route from the McCain home, but couldn't tell their numbers or condition. Soon as he caught sight of the yard he knew it was safe to approach.

Several bodies were lying about, but the fight was over. Charo was outside the house, checking the raiders. Again, it appeared anyone left alive had been helped to make their retreat.

'Missed all the fun, brother dear,' he quipped. 'Were you asleep on the job?'

Stopping his horse, Trace ignored the barb. 'How'd we do? Anyone hurt?'

Charo put his hands on his hips, serious at once. 'Bud took a slug to the right side of his chest – missed his lung, so Ma has hopes it didn't do too much damage. Stoco wasn't so lucky – we lost him in the fight, and Ruban was hit high in the leg. All told, we fared a lot better than we had a right to expect.' He motioned around at the corpses. 'They left six bodies behind and there were a couple of wounded when they high-tailed it back to Eller.'

'The Double K didn't get off that easy. Most of them were wiped out – near as I could tell. I left Melanie to see who all was left alive. Someone was still shooting from the house when I surprised the attackers from behind. I did manage to hit Armando – one of the Eller gang's top men.'

Charo narrowed his gaze. 'Quite a coincidence – Lex Banning riding up the canyon yesterday, and we end up with both ranches being attacked simultaneously. If Lonnie hadn't been out of position from his lookout position, he'd have missed the buzzards slipping through the trees. They expected a lookout on Eagle Point, and they passed by without being in view from there.'

'Same thing for the Kendall place. The two men keeping watch for them were overran right off. If Melanie hadn't been on her way to take them a meal, they would have gotten them all. She flagged me down and I was able to run them off.'

'With the number the raiders lost here and over at Kendall's ranch, it has to put a dent in the Eller fighting force.'

'I don't see them trying to hit our ranch again,' Trace postulated. 'They had to have learned a lesson from this attack. But the Kendall people are out of any fight whatsoever.'

Charo bobbed his head in agreement. 'So, unless the Eller gang tucks their tails and seek a weaker foe elsewhere, they will still hit the town.'

'Yeah, but can we be sure of that?'

'Only if we keep an eye on them,' Charo said. 'Do you want the job, or should I saddle me a horse?'

Trace surveyed the battlefield once more. 'I'll need a fresh mount.'

Shaking his head, Charo displayed a grim smirk. 'I see trouble coming for you as it is.' He tipped his head to the main trail. 'You're going to have your hands full right here for the next few minutes.'

Trace turned in the saddle and watched as Melanie and Randy rode into the yard. Randy had one arm wrapped tightly against his body, obviously having been wounded. He was hunched over the saddle and the pallor of his face revealed he was in pain and possibly shock. Trace climbed down so he and Charo could help Randy dismount.

Melanie had tears in her eyes, but her voice was under control when she spoke.

'Randy is the only one left alive. They killed everyone else.'

'You've come to the right place,' Charo told her. 'We'll have Ma take a look at your brother and see if she thinks he needs the town doctor.'

Melanie had gotten off of her horse as Charo helped Randy to the house. Trace moved over and put his arm around her shoulders, wishing to comfort her. She wasn't satisfied with the modest consoling and turned until she could put her arms around him and rest her head against his shoulder.

He held her close, wishing he knew the words that would aid her sorrow. She wept silently, clinging to him, releasing the fear, agony and terrible loss. There were no comforting words, nothing he could say to ease her pain, so he stood there, regretting his helplessness.

After a few moments, she regained her composure, sniffing back her tears. She pushed herself gently away from his arms and looked up at him.

'Did you lose many of your family?'   she asked, showing concern for him.

'Bud got hit the worst and we lost one man – plus Ruban was hit in the leg.'

'If Ruban and Jose had been at our house, they would likely be dead now too.'

'It was a deadly plan of attack. I'm afraid Lex Banning told them our two ranches would protect the town. I don't see Eller trying to rustle a thousand head of beef and drive them a couple hundred miles to reach a place where he could hope to sell them.'

'You said Lex Banning?'

'Bud spotting him heading out of the valley yesterday in their direction. Either he went to them with some kind of deal or they caught him and got the information they needed about our ranches.'

'But your family drove them off.' She looked around at the dead raiders. 'And you did a lot of damage over at our place. Won't they give up and leave?'

'We don't know what to expect,' Trace admitted. 'We're going to keep an eye on them and try and figure their next move. If they leave the country, we'll be done with them. If not … ?' He sighed. 'We'll deal with whatever they throw at us.'

Trace looked at the two horses she and Randy had arrived on. 'Is

Randy's horse fresh?'

She nodded. 'I took him out of the corral. He's one of our best.'

'And you have some food on your mount?'

Melanie understood. 'I'll put the sandwiches in your saddlebags while you change over your rifle scabbard and fill your canteen.'

Trace quickly got what he needed and took the reins of Randy's horse. He paused, unable to ride away without taking Melanie into his arms. She came willingly and he kissed her gently.

'I'm much better than Charo when it comes to hunting or moving quietly,' he told her. 'I'm the best man to find out what the Eller bunch is going to do.'

'I know,' she said, showing her support. 'Be careful.'

He checked the stirrups for length as he took a seat atop the horse. Randy was nearly as tall as him so no adjustment was need. Then he raised a hand to Melanie in farewell. He took a mental photograph of the way she forced a smile of reinforcement to her face. Then he whirled about and headed down the southern trail.

The way was clear and the tracks easy to read, so Trace kept up a hurried pace. He needed to get as close as possible before Eller had time to put out sentries or watch for anyone on his raiders back-trail. This would be dangerous, but not as dangerous as trying to guess the Eller gang's next move.

***

Trace smelled smoke before he heard the clatter of pans, the whinny of a horse, and the sound of distant voices. Someone was cursing loudly, which helped to gauge how far it was to the camp. The noise allowed him time to stake his horse in a sheltered chaparral, exchange his riding boots for his hunting moccasins, and move forward with as much stealth as possible.

It was late afternoon, and the sun had dipped over the western horizon. Remaining in the shadows, Trace crawled quietly towards the campsite.

It was slow, hot, tedious work, moving along on his stomach. But he inched along until he was able to see much of the bivouac area. He eased through a tangle of vines, holding his breath each time a man's eyes would roam across the surrounding brush or trees.

There were several wounded men being tended to, most suffering from flesh wounds and sitting on ground blankets. A couple were stretched out who had not been so lucky, either dying or already dead.

Trace eased up under some leafy bushes that pretty much hid him from view. He held his breath and tried to make out what was being said.

A silence fell over the group, and he twisted enough to see what was happening.

One man had been positioned next to a fire, covered with a blanket and being treated with special care. Trace recognized him as Armando, the Mexican he had shot at the Double K ranch. Two large, powerfully-built men were standing over him. One of them shook his head.

'He's gone, Hutch,' the big brute said. 'Bullet hit him in the vitals. Nothing we could do.'

'Dammit, Dutch!' the other complained. 'What went wrong? Did that Banning character set us up? Did he lie with his dying breath?'

Dutch looked over at the gunman, Vin Lacy. 'What do you think went wrong?'

'We had them cold at the Kendall place,' he said. 'There was maybe one or two wounded men left in the house. We were about to set fire to it – then some jasper opened up on us from a hill overlooking the yard. Hell of a shooter too. He nailed three or four of our guys and hit Armando as we were making a break to escape.'

'Only one man?' Dutch challenged. 'One man killed so many?'

'It could have been Charo,' Enrico guessed from a short distance away. 'Anyone who can put out candles with a handgun could sure enough do some damage with a rifle.'

Hutch reached down and pulled the blanket over Armando's lifeless eyes. 'Whoever did this, I want him dead.'

'He was the first man to ride with us,' Dutch seconded his vow. 'He has done a dozen raids for us, and he never once failed to do the job.'

'Armando was a good leader,' Vin joined in with the praise. 'All of the men respected him.'

'What about the other ranch?' Dutch asked Enrico Gomez, the one he had put in charge of the second attack. 'How did we lose so many men?'

'The house was built like a fortress,' Enrico whined. 'We hit it with everything we had, but the rock walls protected them. There was no decent cover from which to fight. We had to pull back or lose more of our men. '

Dutch put his hands on his hips and stared at his fallen comrade on the ground. His face was a mask of hate, his teeth tightly set. He looked mad enough to take on a full-grown grizzly – and give the bear first bite.

'That weasel from town must have lied to us!' he snarled the words.

'Cuerdo worked on him for an hour,' Hutch countered his statement. 'No one could have lied after such treatment. He was begging for death long before his end.'

'The guy admitted he'd never seen the McCain ranch,' Vin pointed out. 'He probably didn't know it was built like a fort.'

'So we do nothing?' Hutch asked. 'We let this man who killed Armando go on living?'

'After the town falls,' Vin said tightly, 'I'll find Charo on my own. I'll collect for the death of our friend.'

Hutch looked at his brother. 'Vin is right. We came to take the town. It has cost us a lot of men, but we have eliminated the support of the ranches. The one place was wiped out, and we're sure to have killed a few of them in the attack on the McCain place. That means the town is sitting there with only a handful of storekeepers, farmers, and old men. We can take what we want.'

Dutch finally gave an affirmative nod. 'Yes, we take what we want – then we level Rio Blanco! It will be a dire warning to any future towns we decide to hit.'

'Put out a couple guards – those who are injured and can't ride with us tomorrow. Have everyone else get plenty of food and rest. Come sunup, we will ride to Rio Blanco and make a statement that all Texas will understand – resist the will of the Ellers and you will die hard deaths!'

***

Trace had managed to get away unseen, but it was midnight before he reached the house. Even as he entered the yard, a man with a gun challenged him. He recognized Dean when he spoke up.

'That you Trace?'

'It's me,' he said. 'I'm about done in. Got anything hot to eat?'

Ma has a kettle of chili on the stove, along with coffee. With us still guarding the place, we've got people going an coming at all hours.'

'You take care of the Kendalls?'

'Randy is in the bunkhouse, Melanie is sharing a room with Tish, and we sent a couple men over to bury Harvey and his men, including the two who were on guard. They dumped the gang members in a ditch altogether. Did the same thing here. Stuck a sign on their plot of ground listing the number of men buried there. Didn't bother with a cross.'

'No, God will hand out their final judgment. I'm not one to pine or pray over depraved animals who rob and kill women and children.'

'Likewise,' Dean said. 'They chose to do the deeds – they deserve no forgiveness from anyone this side of heaven.'

'I've got news and it is going to mean another fight. Soon as I get something to eat, we need to have a meeting.'

'Go on and grab a bite. I'll put up your horse and wake the house.'

Trace had finished eating by the time Dean had woke the other members of the family. Everyone gathered in the living room. Glancing about, the homestead looked in pretty good shape, other than for a few bullet holes in the interior walls. Those rounds had mostly come through the open windows.

Melanie offered Trace a sleepy smile, glad to see he had returned safely. Trace hadn't intended to wake everyone, but the women and even the wounded Randy and Ruban were crowded into the room.

'What's up, Trace?' Charo asked, his shirt untucked and his hair mussed. 'Couldn't this wait until morning?'

Trace waited until everyone was in the room and ready to listen. He couldn't meet Tish Banning's eyes, so he addressed the others.

'Eller is fixing to hit the town tomorrow. I wasn't able to get their numbers, because the camp was spread out some. I would guess twenty or more men, but I only saw one Indian. I remember someone saying they often have several in their gang, so they probably had a camp of their own. The raiders talked like they had plenty of men to do the job and they intend to kill every man, woman and child, then burn Rio Blanco to the ground.'

The words were like an icy ring, freezing every person in the room. No one said anything right off, so Trace continued, knowing the next words would be painful to hear.

'The bandits captured Lex Banning,' He decided to save Tish some grief. 'I heard them talking, and they tortured him to get everything he knew out of him. He gave them the strength of the town, and the location of our ranches ... before he died.'

Tish sucked in her breath, but she did not cry out. Lonnie put his arm around her shoulders and pulled her in close.

'I am also partly to blame for the Ellers rage. When I was trying to drive away the bandits from the Kendall place, I shot the Mexican who had threatened us in town. Turns out, he and the Eller brothers were very close. They'll be looking to get even with me as well.'

'How do they know it was you?' Charo asked.

'They assumed it was either me or you.'

'That means they will come here after they destroy the town,' Lonnie said. 'We'll have to be ready to take them on again.'

'Without us, the town doesn't stand a chance,' Trace pointed out.

Dean shook his head. 'They don't have much of a chance with us either. It would take a hundred men to protect Rio Blanco, sprawled out like it is. With no more than the handful of able men in town, they won't last ten minutes. Even with our help, they wouldn't last an hour.'

Charo said: 'Not to mention, we're going to have to be ready here at home. Now that they've seen the house, they will have a plan – maybe fire or explosives – but they won't be caught unaware like those first attackers.'

'We can warn them,' Lonnie suggested. 'Get them to join us here. With another dozen men, we would easily battle the bandit gang to a standstill.'

'Those people have invested their lives and futures in their homes and businesses,' Melanie interposed. 'We can't ask them to simply abandon everything they've worked for and watch it go up in smoke.'

'Things don't count for much when the lives of your family is in the pot,' Dean said. 'Most of them can start again.'

Trace waited while the others in the room said their peace. When it grew silent, he spoke in a cool, collected voice. 'I'll be going to town at first light. We can change a few defensive positions and prepare for the Ellers.'

'It's suicide!' Lonnie argued. 'If Gramps was back with his newly hired men, we might have enough strength to withstand a siege, but two or three added guns won't be enough to make a difference.'

'What do you say, Charo?' Dean asked the gunfighter of the family.

Charo frowned in thought. 'I'm not one to run from a fight, but I sure would like an even draw. Bud is out of action, and we still don't know if he'll pull through. I want to get even with those snakes for the attack on our ranch, but I don't want to get killed.'

'Want to sum that up to an actual answer?' Lonnie ribbed him.

Charo lifted his shoulders. 'Simple – I'm for fighting, but not for getting killed.'

Dean snorted his disdain. 'I think all of us here feel the same way.'

'You have to have enough men to ward off any attack,' Trace told Dean. 'That means keeping most of the men here on the ranch.'

'But you won't have a chance in town, Trace!' Melanie blurted out. 'What good will dying do?'

Ma McCain had not said a word. Now she rose up from her chair to speak. Her eyes traversed over her boys, their hired help, and the two girls in the room. Dean's wife was absent, for she was sitting with Bud.

'I reckon I can speak for Gramps,' – she always called Sod Gramps, even though he was a father-in-law to her – and I usually take his side in major decisions. Dean has pointed out that, if Gramps and his help were here, we would have enough to help the townspeople put up a good fight. I have to agree with Dean. Them folks who want to live can come here and stay with us until the Ellers gang leaves the country. If they refuse to desert their homes or businesses, they will have to fight for them. I won't make any demands of any of you. If you choose to ride in with Trace, we'll get by with however many of us there are left. I don't want to see any of you hurt, but you're grown men, and able to make up your own minds. I want you to know, I'll support whatever decision you make.'

The room fell to total silence. As if to punctuate her lengthy speech, Ma McCain walked out of the room, heading for a bed and a fitful night's sleep.

Dean held his tongue until they heard the door to his mother's room close. 'All right,' he said quietly. 'Ma has put it up to each of us as to what we will do.' He looked at Trace. 'Make the people the offer to come here for their safety. Soon as help arrives, we'll drive that pack of vermin out of the country or kill them all.'

Trace took a deep breath, then let it out slowly. He had made up his own mind. His conscience could accept only one decision.

'I'll make the offer,' he said, but I know most of those people won't change their minds. If it was my home, I would leave either.'

'So you're going to stand with them against Eller's Marauders.'

Dean made it a statement, requiring no reply. However, he got one from Melanie.

'I'm going with Trace,' she stated without question. 'I'm not a great shot with a rifle, but I can load for Trace or one of the others.' She looked at Randy, before he could object.

'Doc Myer brought me into the world, and I've been the best of friends with Martha Tibbs all of my life. I won't let them face this alone.'

'Count me in,' Randy said. 'I feel the same as my sister.'

Trace didn't argue, even though he hated the thought of putting the two of them in danger. Besides which, they weren't his to command, and Melanie was right about having someone help load guns. He said, 'We'll leave at sunup. That should give us three or four hours to get ready, before the raiders reach town. Plus, any who have the good sense to leave will have time to get away.'

'Reckon I'll tag along,' Charo said. 'That fellow, Vin Lacy will be looking for me. I'd hate for the guy to get eye strain from not being able to find me. Between Trace and me, we'll cut the odds down real quick.'

Trace couldn't help but smile. 'With you along, it practically gives us the advantage!'

Several people in the room laughed, but it was a taut, strained mirth. The shadow of death loomed very heavy, a foreboding of impending adversity.

Chapter Nine

Barney Cod was standing guard at a crude barricade the town had thrown up across one end of the main street. He pushed a small cart to one side to open the path for the McCains and Kendalls to enter, then closed the opening behind them.

'Lyle was keeping watch a ways down the valley and thought he heard shots yesterday,' the sheriff said. 'From the bandage on Randy's arm, I'd say he was right.'

Randy could not hide his grief. 'Wiped us out, Barney. We're all that's left of the Double K.'

Barney's shoulders drooped. 'Damn, I thought we should have sent a few men to try and help.'

'You would have been too late,' Melanie told him. 'If I hadn't gotten Trace to help, Randy would have died too. And we were only five minutes away.'

'They hit our place at the same time,' Trace explained. 'I happened to be closer to the Kendall place than my own. Knowing we had the better chance to defend our house, I went with Melanie to do what I could.'

Barney looked up at Charo. 'How did you fair at the McCain ranch?'

'We cut the odds a little,' Charo said. 'I don't think we'll be next on the Ellers list; we're pretty certain it will be you – a couple of hours from now.'

Trace surveyed the town, noting the long distances between some of the houses, with huge gaps that ran between some of the larger buildings. With the exception of the barn, where the dances were held, there wasn't a defensible building in town.

'I'd appreciate you gathering the people together, Barney,' Trace spoke to the sheriff. 'I'd like to have a few words with everyone.'

The four of them remained seated on their horses, while Barney raised the alarm to get everyone in the city square. Men and women came tramping out from every house or building. Trace didn't have to count them, knowing their number would be near fifty – counting all of the children. Picking out the men who could fight, and the few women among them who knew how to shoot, he came up with a number under twenty. It wasn't much of an army to defend an entire town.

Barney started things off, explaining about the twin raids yesterday and the outcome. He finished with: 'Randy and Melanie are all that's left from the Kendall place. The McCains are in better shape, but Trace here wants to speak to you.'

The crowd was silent, somber, with no hostility showing on their faces now. They were scared, uncertain, and needed someone to take charge and give orders. Barney knew nothing about this kind of battle, and no Confederate officers had returned from the war. The couple who had served were about the only seasoned fighters, but they had families to worry about.

'I slipped up on the bandit camp last night,' Trace informed the group. 'The Eller brothers were busy outlining their attack for today.' He grunted. 'They intend to level the town and kill every single one of you ... not even sparing the children.'

The news shook many of them to their heels, some muttering under their breath, and others praying for deliverance from such bandits. All of them were aware of their chances, and those were certainly not good.

'There's a possibility the raiders might send a part of their force to hit our ranch, to keep us from being able to help protect the town. So we have to keep men there to defend the place. Bud is too severely wounded to move, and my mother won't leave his side. Me and Charo are as much help as you're going to get from our ranch.'

'Barney said you might have an offer of some kind?' Lyle spoke up.

'We can put all of you up at the ranch,' Trace said. 'Sod McCain is due back any day with men he is hiring for roundup. Could be as many as ten or twelve. Without extra guns, the odds aren't good.'

'You want us to abandon the town?' Lyle was incredulous. 'Let them burn the place down, along with everything we've worked for all these years?'

'What I'm saying is, we can defend the ranch, because it's only three buildings and they are grouped together. This town is spread over five acres. The raiders can come in from every direction but up. It's going to be nearly impossible to defend it against such a large fighting force.'

'Heck, McCain,' Lyle said. 'You would have us start over from scratch – and I still owe money for supplies and groceries that are on my shelves.'

'Maybe just the women and children?' Melanie suggested. 'We don't have to risk their lives.'

'I'm not leaving my husband – nor my home either,' Martha said without hesitation. 'I can shoot a gun, and I sure know how to load one. I'm not running from that scum.'

Her vow brought a rumble of approval.

Trace straightened up in the saddle. 'I'm just here to make the offer. Our place is the most sturdy and safest route. I wanted you to know the only two options we've got.'

'Two options?' Barney queried.

'Yes. Run or fight.'

Lyle looked around the group, then back at Trace. 'Looks like we're all agreed, McCain. We are gonna fight.'

'How about getting some of the children to safety?' Melanie

wanted to know.

Charo didn't allow anyone to answer, pointing to a dust cloud about a mile distant. 'Looks like we don't have as much time as we'd hoped. There appears to be a big herd of trouble headed this way.'

'Get your guns!' Barney shouted. 'Get the kids to cover!'

'Let's take the barn!' Charo hollered over the noise and excitement. 'Unless they set fire to it, the walls are built out of thick slabs of wood. Ought to be enough to stop a good many bullets.'

Trace didn't have to give any order, as Melanie and Randy were already heading towards the sturdy structure. Being the first building at the south end of town, it would be an important objective for the Eller gang. The few men who were lining up to defend the barricade would be of little help defending the barn.

'Once inside, we've no place to retreat to,' Trace told Charo.

Charo laughed, his eyes dancing with fervor. 'Since when does a McCain retreat from a fight, Trace? We'll cut them down as fast as they come at us.'

Trace grumbled: 'Remind me to pick my own spot to defend next time.'

***

Hutch Eller held up his hand, stopping his men. With narrow, steady eyes, he regarded the flimsy-built defense that had been thrown up to ward off the impending attack. His thin lips curled into a cruel smile.

'Look at that, my brother,' he scoffed to Dutch. 'The town is an open invitation. How can so few people think they have a chance against us?'

'Spread out like it is, they might as well have put out tables with punch bowls and pastries for us,' Dutch replied.

'They might have a couple decent shooters,' Vin warned. 'We ought to circle to the sides and avoid charging right at their strength.'

'You said there were only about a dozen men on the street, when you and Armando visited?'

'And the one McCain. He probably helped defend their ranch, so we know he can shoot.'

'Send the Indians to the right. They can take control of the big barn. You take a few men to the left and come at them from that side. The rest of us will bust through their barricade and ride over their dying bodies!'

Vin accepted the order, waved to Cuerdo and motioned for him to lead the renegades in an attack on the barn. Then he took several men and began to circle to the east side of town.

Hutch and Dutch remained seated like two generals, waiting for their army to get into position, so they could give the order to charge.

'Today, we get even for the death of Armando and so many of our men,' Hutch hissed through his clenched teeth.

'Keep low and let the others ride ahead of you,' Dutch warned. 'If they have a couple of marksmen, we don't want to be their first targets.'

'We will show all of Texas not to stand against us,' Hutch boasted. 'After we smash these people into the dust, no one will dare oppose Eller's Marauders!'

***

From his place near the door of the barn, Trace watched the party of men split into groups. He checked his Henry rifle once more and made sure his ammunition was at hand. Charo was at the lone window and Randy was up in the loft with Melanie to load for him.

'I make the count at about forty men, including a dozen or so Indians,' Charo said. 'Looks like we are the target of the renegades.'

'From their outfits, I'd say they are Comanche and Apache, with maybe a straggler or two from other tribes. Never saw a misfit bunch like this gang before.'

'Almost like Comancheros,' Charo said. 'Except they are usually mostly Mexicans and halfbreed outlaws.'

'Watch them close,' Trace warned. 'Those Indians will try to sneak up on us. Keep track of as many as you can.'

'Odds aren't too bad,' Charo said flippantly. 'Only twenty to one – for the two of us. Whatever the rest of the town gets will be gravy.'

Trace grunted. 'That's nice to know. But if you get lucky and finish your half first, I'll let you help me with the rest.'

As they watched, the dozen or so Indians left their horses at a hundred yards and began filtering through the sparse brush and few cedars on that side of the barn. From the front, the Eller boys had lined up with a wide space between each man. It would be more difficult for a poor shot to hit anyone, because a miss was a miss – no chance at hitting a man close by or behind the target.

'I wonder how Bud is doing this morning,' Charo said to break the strained silence.

Trace grunted. 'I doubt he's in any more danger of dying that we are.'

Charo grinned. 'I've said some mean, sarcastic things to you a time or two.'

'Yeah, you surely have.'

'Well, just in case something happens to one of us, I'd like you to know – I meant every word I said!'

Trace chuckled. 'And I'd like you to know, the only regret I have is not getting around to putting a good beating on you. I missed a lot of chances when we were growing up, and now ...'

'Yeah,' was Charo's soft reply.

A single gunshot was fired into the air, by a big man with red hair and beard, signaling the attack. The skirmish line charged from the front, while another group came at them from the east side. The Indians began shooting and trying to maneuver closer to the barn.

Trace concentrated on a single man. When he moved – bang! -- he dropped, mortally wounded. Then Trace targeted to a second Indian, finding the ones closest first. Three times he knocked his man down, as Charo hit another one. He was best at close range with a handgun, but was no slouch with a rifle.

Bullets chipped wood off of the door and slapped into the walls of the barn, but the Indians were growing more wary, seeing their companions fall. They began to crawl from one hiding spot to another presenting almost no target for a shooter.

Trace turned his attention to the storming charge from the front of the blockade. The bandits were mingled into a driving, raging mass of humanity, amongst swirling dust, twisting, rearing horses, and smoke, lead and fire-spitting guns.

'Help the barricade!' Trace called to his brother.

Charo discarded his rifle and took a pistol in either hand. He began to fire as fast as he could find targets, knocking three or four men off of their horses.

Trace took out two more Indians and they stopped their advance. Starting out with a dozen, six of their number were out of the fight. They decided to back away and let the other two groups take the barn.

Randy was firing from above and he was a fair shot. He hit a couple of riders out of his first five or six shots. It wasn't enough as the bandits swept over the blockade, their horses shouldering the carts and wagons aside. Trace saw two of the townsmen go down under the raiders' blazing guns. He managed to draw a bead on one of the men who'd help kill them. The rifle bucked against his shoulder and the man was gone, lost among the thundering hooves of the horses.

Time was lost in the hectic panic of the moment, gunblasts mixed with screams of pain or terror. Several of the remaining townspeople risked death to cross the street, some women with children running for their very lives. Randy called out to them to retreat to the barn and many came running.

Trace and Charo gave them as much cover as they could, but Trace had to switch to his handgun when he ran out of ammo.

Charo called out he had to reload and paused to toss his rifle to Trace. His lighter Winchester was easy to use and Trace quickly knocked over two of the attackers.

Lyle reached the door, but was knocked to the ground by a bullet in his upper back. Martha pulled and tugged at him, until Trace braved the gunfire and helped drag him inside the shelter of the barn.

Doc Myer, his wife, and several more children came in through the back of the barn. Two other men from the barricade set up a covering fire at the rear door. It allowed more people to enter, as the bandits systematically drove men from their cover into the barn. They were being herded into the pen for slaughter, and there was nothing they could do about it. Doc took his gun and helped to hold the rear door, while Tibbs crawled up front. He had been wounded in the leg, but he was still able to shoot.

'Did you manage to get word out? Is there any chance of help getting here?' Charo asked him.

The man shook his head. 'They cut the telegraph wires the day Armando showed up to threaten us. Doc Myer's boy rode for help yesterday, but he couldn't possible get back for a couple days. We'll never hold till then.'

'Ever wonder what those boys thought at the Alamo that last day?' Charo asked no one in particular.

'I believe I do,' Tibbs was the one to reply. 'If they set fire to this place, we'll all be roasted alive.'

The shooting died down, the bandits slowly working their way to surround the barn. Although the Indians had run off, one was left who dressed in regular clothes. Trace tried to get a bead on him, but he was too smart. He kept moving rapidly from cover to cover, not exposing himself in the least. With so many others now involved in the assault on the barn, Trace dismissed the man.

The shooting had died down, the bandits slowly working their way into position for the final kill. They were confident, smelling victory. The townspeople were like rabbits in a trap, unable to run. It was only a matter of time – and everyone on both sides knew it.

Trace cast a longing glance at the loft. Randy still fired a shot periodically, so he knew the Kendalls were still in the fight.

'I love you, Melanie,' he whispered. 'I promise to tell you that the next time I see you – even if it isn't in this lifetime!'

Children were crying, as were many of the women. The men had tears in their eyes too, from their lack of strength or numbers to protect their town and family. This barn had once been for celebration, or praise to God, a fun and spiritual place. Now the straw-covered dance floor was littered with bodies and puddles of blood from the wounded or dying. The parson was praying, holding hands with a couple of the elderly women and many of the children. All of those people would die without ever hurting a soul.

Trace gritted his teeth in anger. He was so utterly helpless! He had only one gun, and he would fight until his last breath, but it would not be enough. Charo would be there at his side, dealing out as much justice as he could with his guns. The two of them would take a lot of the bandits with them, but the end was near. There simply wasn't enough –

'Hey!' Charo exclaimed. 'Take a look over there on the hill!'

Trace peered across the dusty street, looking beyond the barricade. He made out several men, all on foot, and all coming as fast as they could toward the edge of town.

'That's Dean in front!' Charo said. 'Looks like most of the boys came in from the ranch too!'

Trace took a position next to Charo. 'We need to distract Eller's gang long enough for Dean and the others to get here. If they don't make it past the barricade, we'll all be dead.'

Charo chortled. 'Let's give those buzzards a taste of McCain vengeance!'

Trace turned to the others in the barn. 'Every man who can shoot -- other than those watching the back door -- get over here on the double!'

Barney limped over, blood still visible on his leg from a bullet crease. There were three men with him besides the doctor.

'We're going to fake a counterattack,' Trace told them shortly. 'Load your weapons!'

'Attack?' Barney couldn't believe it. We're going to do what?'

'Help is coming,' Trace said, tipping his head toward Dean and the others. 'But we need to charge the bandits. If we're convincing enough, they might break off the attack long enough to regroup. That's all we need -- stall their advance for a couple minutes. Then we scoot back here.'

'It'll likely get us all killed!' Barney complained, but he was loading his gun.

Trace took Tibbs's handgun, so he was loaded in either hand, as was Charo. They took a position next to the door, waiting until all of the men were ready.

'Keep low, keep moving and shooting. Use what cover you can find. We only have to confuse Eller's men long enough for the help to get to the barn.'

Barney looked across the the way, blinked in surprise, and allowed himself a grim smile. 'I see your plan now. Get their backs exposed to the other McCains long enough to get them into the fight. Then we retreat with a better chance of holding out inside the barn.'

'We might get lucky and drive the bunch of mangy coyotes off like we did the Indians. They cut and ran, once we whittled down their number.'

Randy had come down from the loft to join them. Melanie was still shooting to keep up the ruse of a defense. The group led by Vin was still held off at the back door, so many of Eller's fighters were not in position to take on a frontal assault.

Randy had a pistol in his good hand. 'I'll give you six shots of support,' he vowed. 'Then I'll have to duck for cover.'

'Same goes for everyone,' Trace warned. 'We charge and drive them back as much as possible, but when you run out of ammo, retreat for the barn. First men back, reload and cover the retreat of everyone else. Standing around to reload would get some of us killed … and we can't afford the loss of firepower.'

'That's right,' Charo put in. 'Anyone who gets killed get's a swift kick in the hindquarters! No one dies – understood?'

All gathered at the barn entrance. Then, with battle cries and rebel yells, they charged out the door, all of them shooting as they ran.

Charo and Trace matched each other in speed, trying to find targets as they bolted forward. Bullets kicked up dirt at their feet, cut the wind past their heads and screamed through the flesh of two of the group. Still they attacked as if lost to a frenzy, knocking down several raiders with well-aimed shots.

The sudden assault caught the bandit gang by surprise. Many gave ground, alarmed by the fury of the townsmen's charge. A couple of them were cut down from behind when they broke and ran. At the same time, Dean and the other few men from the ranch attacked from the other side of the street. They fired their guns as they stormed forward. The combination was more than Eller's men were prepared for. They had thought they were the ones on offense, and now the tide had turned. Many of them pulled back, and a few more went down in a hail of bullets.

The battle raged violently and deadly, and Eller's men – not being trained soldiers – began to flee so hastily that they almost trampled over one another. The engagement turned into chaos, as the two Eller's bellowing orders did not slow the retreat.

Trace stopped near the general store seeing the bandits riding away from town. He caught sight of the two redheaded men and carefully sent his last round at the one closest. The man jerked upright from being hit, but kept riding for the open country and safety from the surprise attack. The men around back were powerless to stop the panic and retreated as well. Within moments, every bandit who could ride had left town.

'They'll be back,' Charo said, having come up next to Trace. 'And there's gonna be a tongue lashing like them boys never had before.'

'Yes,' Trace concurred. 'When they have time to reflect on it, they'll know they still had us heavily outnumbered.'

'Did you see Lacy?'

'He was the last to leave, cussing his men's cowardice every step of the way. Unfortunately, my guns were empty. I never got off a shot at him.'

'Too bad.'

'Stopping the Indians helped us immensely,' Trace said returning to the battle itself. 'They couldn't get to the barn. If we had lost that stronghold, we'd have been done. Instead, the few remaining braves took off like spooked cats.'

'Yep,' Charo chuckled. 'Kind of glad I brought you along. You about drove them back single-handed. I always said you were as good with a rifle as I am with a handgun.'

Dean wandered over to stand with them, as the others helped the wounded back to the barn. He was out of breath from the charge, his smoking gun still in his hand.

'You old married men tend to get winded easily,' Charo ribbed him.

'It's more from being dumbfounded at you two's lack of concern for your lives. Whose lunatic idea was that rebel charge?'

'Hey, it worked, didn't it?' Charo said. 'If Eller's men had seen you over there, they would have turned their guns on you and mowed you down like a scythe cutting wheat.'

'We had to do something unexpected,' Trace said. 'A surprise attack was all I could think of.'

Dean looked at the bodies strewn about in the street. A couple of men who had charged with them were among the dead, and another two were wounded. Randy had also been grazed, but it was above the knee on his bad leg, so it wouldn't slow him down from his usual snail's pace.

Charo had a gash along his left arm and had lost his hat. Trace was a little shocked that neither he nor his two-gun brother had been seriously wounded. Counting Dean and the three or four from the ranch, they had nine fighting men left. A couple others could shoot but weren't mobile.

'Any idea how many got away?' Charo asked.

Trace shook his head. 'Can't be sure, but I'd say between fifteen to twenty.'

'Dad-blame-it! I know you and me shot a dozen or more,' he complained. 'Can't anyone else around here shoot?'

'If the Indians have run off, it will help,' Trace observed. 'The only one left is the one who dresses like the rest of the bandits. Wouldn't know he's Indian, except he wears an Indian headband to keep his long hair in place.'

Dean finally holstered his gun. He looked at his brothers with a serious expression. 'There ain't but Ma, Lonnie and Ruban out at the place. That is, of the people who can shoot. Bud was awake, so we put him next to a window, but my wife and Tish have never fired a gun. If Eller decides to hit the place … ' He didn't have to finish.

'I'm betting they will be too busy gathering their men. If we're lucky, they will decide it's too expensive to try again.'

'I don't know, Trace,' Dean said. 'Look around. We're down to a mere handful to protect the barn. When they come back, they will almost certainly set fire to the rest of the town. Maybe we ought to take everyone to the ranch.'

'Several of the wounded couldn't make a journey that far,' Trace replied. 'Plus, they didn't fight this hard to give up their homes or the town. My guess, they will try and scout us to learn our numbers, then hit us as hard as they can.'

'With so few of us, I don't see how we can hold the town.'

'Let's put a couple men on guard and discuss ideas,' Trace said. 'The ladies who aren't helping the wounded can fix a meal – might be our last chance to eat in quite some time.'

'Yeah, like forever,' Dean said dejectedly.

Chapter Ten

Hutch Eller fumed in a hushed silence, most of the men afraid to even whisper to one another. There was no fire, no hint of a meal, and most faces were long and strained. Defeat was not common to this band of men, but they had suffered two setbacks in a row from the people of Rio Blanco.

Stopping his angry pace around the group of men, he stopped to stare at his brother. Dutch had taken a slug in the back during their retreat. Cuerdo had worked on him for a few minutes, but it was hopeless. Dutch's haggard breath came to a sudden stop; the man was dead.

'Too much blood loss inside of him,' the Indian said. 'Removing the bullet did no good.'

Hutch swore vehemently, cursing the townspeople, their children, their animals, even their pets! He wanted revenge and he wanted it now!

'How many men did you count against us?' he asked Vin Lacy.

'It was tough to tell,' Vin said with open distaste. 'There were so many of our men running for their lives. I had a hard time even gauging the size of the town's force. I had to get out or get trampled during the retreat.'

'I saw the second group – no more than six men. There couldn't have been any more than that in their crazy charge from the barn. Our gang of deadly killers,' Hutch snarled sarcastically, 'our band of deadly raiders, the men who bring terror to the entire southwest – they turned like so many chickens from a single fox!'

'Do we forget Rio Blanco?' Enrico asked, having gained Armando's position in the gang. 'The Indians are gone. They deserted Cuerdo when they lost half of their number. A couple of those protecting the town are very good shots.'

'They killed Armando and my brother!' Hutch roared. 'Do you expect me to turn tail and run – like the rest of your worthless dogs!'

'It'll be dark in another hour,' Vin interrupted, casting a skyward glance. 'I can slip in close and take a look-see at what we're up against. The charge was desperation, to help get their reinforcements to the barn. But, like you, Hutch, I saw only a handful of men.'

'They were shooting like a hundred men,' Enrico pointed out. 'Half of our men are dead and many more are wounded. We have less than twenty men for an attack. If we couldn't do it with over forty men – counting the Indians – how can we defeat them with so few men?'

Vin looked around, studying the raddled faces, noting the many men who were sporting bandages of one kind or another. They weren't the same army as the one they had started with. It had been a costly campaign, including the price of Dutch Eller. With him gone, his brother would never quit. He wanted everyone in Rio Blanco dead.

But he knew another attack would be a gamble. If they lost half of their men again, those remaining would desert the gang. Hutch needed a victory so they could recruit more followers. And Cuerdo would have to find more renegades for their ranks. The Indians added a measure of fear whenever they attacked a settlement or ranch. Little Bend had whet their appetites for pillaging a town. They knew there was food and drink, money, valuables and women to be had. They had lined their pockets with everything of value, taken what they pleased, then burned or destroyed the rest.

There had been no major opposition in Little Bend. The few men had scattered, taking their wives and children. The few who escaped had spread the tale – the legend of the Eller Marauders had taken form.

Such was not the case with Rio Blanco. As he looked off towards the valley, he decided the single difference was the McCains. If they were to defeat the town, they had to first defeat the McCains themselves!

***

Trace patrolled the town alone. Dean and Randy took turns in the loft of the barn and Charo manned the barricade. It wasn't much of a defense, but everyone was in need of rest. The wounded were being treated, the children fed and put in makeshift beds for the night. They had no choice but to remain in the barn, for it was Rio Blanco's last defense.

If Eller came at them again, it would be the death of them all. They couldn't hope to hold out against twenty or more men for any length of time. Except for himself and Charo, not one of the defenders was even an accomplished hunter. He and his brother had to carry the brunt of the load, and their luck would not hold forever.

Going through the Tibbs store, Trace paused at the back door, looking up towards the distant hills. It would be dark soon. Eller had likely regrouped and was planning his final assault. Trace wondered how he would come at them. Certainly not a frontal attack like last time. That had cost him too many men. If they set fire to the town, the bandits would burn up any loot or supplies they hoped to steal. But it would certainly be the end for the townspeople, as would setting fire to the barn.

The weariness saturated his bones, causing Trace to sit down against the wall, still able to see out the open back door, but needing to rest for a minute. He was exhausted, emotionally and physically. The furious days of fighting, running, scouting, and standing constant guard had worn him to a frazzle. It was all he could do to keep his eyes open.

Something moved behind him –

Trace immediately grabbed his gun and whirled about, ready to shoot!

Melanie sucked in her breath at his reaction, stopping dead in her tracks. 'I'm sorry!' she gasped. 'I saw the open door, but didn't see you sitting there.'

Trace lowered his gun at once. 'Boy, kitten,' he apologized, 'I about put a slug in you. Don't be sneaking around like that.'

'I wasn't sneaking,' Melanie corrected, coming over to settle down on the floor next to him. 'I was looking for you. Were you asleep?'

'I wish,' he said. 'I'm on guard duty, but I can hardly keep my eyes open.'

Melanie put a hesitant hand on his arm. 'You are so very worn out, Trace. You need to rest, or you'll be no good if we are attacked again.'

Trace marveled that the girl could look so fresh, so vibrant, after the long, hard-fought battle. There was a smudge on her cheek, a stain of someone's blood on the hem of her skirt, but she was alert and beautiful.

'Did I hear right? Did you call me *kitten* just now?'

He frowned, not remembering. 'Did I?' Maybe I'm more tired than I thought.'

Melanie leaned against him, resting her head against his shoulder. 'Why would you call me that?'

'I don't know,' he answered truthfully. 'Maybe it's because you remind me of a soft, cuddly kitten, begging to be picked up and loved on.'

'And have my ears scratched?' she teased.

Trace put his hand under her chin, tipping her face towards his. 'No,' he whispered, 'to be kissed.'

And he did just that.

***

Trace awoke with a start, coming erect from where he'd been sitting and leaning against the wall. He'd somehow let himself fall asleep!

'Hush!' Melanie shushed him, her hand quickly over to cover his mouth.

Trace blinked to clear his vision and get his brain functioning, then stared out the open door, into the full darkness of the night. Melanie removed her hand and leaned close to him.

'Someone's out there,' she barely breathed. 'I heard him just a moment ago.'

Trace eased up to his feet, using a hand to gently coerce Melanie to stand behind him. His keen hearing picked up the sound of softly padding feet, and he moved a step closer to the door.

'Slip back to the barn. Tell everyone to keep a sharp eye,' he whispered to her.

Once she had left the store, Trace pinpointed where the sound was coming from, then eased out into the darkness. He wished he had his moccasins, but they were packed in his saddlebags – wherever they might be.

He stuck within the darkest shadows next to the building and picked up the sounds once more. He carefully strained his hearing and decided it was a single set of feet. It occurred to him that a single scout might be trying to get a count of fighting men and their positions. Taking a deep breath to try and control his rapid heartbeat, he moved to a position behind where the lone man was heading.

Then, quite without warning, the phantom appeared – a dark outline in front of the alley that ran

between the store and the jail. He was not one of the townspeople, and he had not pulled the gun from his holster. Pointing his Henry at the man's back, he readied himself.

'Don't get twitchy, friend,' he warned him icily. He tightened his finger on the trigger as the man tensed. Any sudden move and he would shoot. Slowly, deliberately, the man lifted his hands well above his shoulders.

'Where do we go from here?' the man asked, as casual like as if needing directions to the nearest barber.

'Start up the street,' Trace ordered. 'Keep your hands held high, and don't do anything sudden-like.

'You're calling the shots, mister,' the man replied.

'That's right, and it would only take one from this Henry I've got trained on you.'

They marched up the middle of the street, not stopping until Dean challenged them from the loft.

'Got a night hawk here,' Trace called out. 'We're coming in.'

'Come ahead, Trace,' Dean said. 'I'll be right down.'

Trace marched his prisoner into the dimly lit barn. He stopped just inside the door, shutting it behind them. It didn't surprise him that the man he'd brought in was Vin Lacy.

Charo had been sleeping, for his eyes were red and he moved stiffly. He ventured over and took a look at the Eller gang's top gun.

'What are you prowling around for?' he asked pointedly. 'Didn't have enough guts to face us during the light of day?'

A glimmer of fire lit up Vin's eyes. 'You're Charo?'

Trace stepped over and lifted the man's gun from its holster. He watched his brother's reaction, knowing this man was his nemesis, his to deal with.

Charo looked Vin over from head to foot. 'Vin Lacy,' he deduced. 'I somehow thought you would look tougher.'

'Few men look tough with their hands in the air,' Vin sparred back. 'Give me my gun and an even chance – then we'll see who's tough.'

'You didn't answer my question. Why the sneaking around in the dark?'

Vin relaxed outwardly, as if being in a life-or-death situation was something he enjoyed. His eyes traversed the room, then returned to Charo.

'I was gonna take a tally of your menfolk. Pretty puny-looking bunch you've got here.'

'We've given more than we've taken from you,' Charo replied. 'Were our ranks full of young fighting men, instead of old-timers, cripples and family men, we'd have plum wiped you out.'

Vin nodded. 'Actually, if it wasn't for you McCains, this town would be rubble and ashes by now. You boys are something we didn't count on.'

'You were warned to stay away,' Charo reminded him. 'It was your band who started this, not us.'

'Trouble is, Charo, you made a big mistake today. One of you killed Dutch Eller.' He sighed to make his point. 'Ain't no way to bounce back from that kind of mistake.'

'The mistake was in not killing you and both Ellers today.'

Trace moved over in front of Vin. 'You chose this fight. I warned you not to test us. The deaths of Armando and Dutch are on you.'

Vin smiled. 'So you were the single gun who showed up to try and save the Kendall ranch.' It was a statement. 'Killed several of our men, including Armando.' He gave a short whistle. 'Very impressive shooting.'

'You saw how well your Indian pals did this morning,' Charo jumped back into the conversation. 'That was me and Trace. How many of them are in your camp now – any at all?'

'Tell you what,' Trace offered. 'How about we stop all of the unnecessary killing? You and Eller against me and my brother. We face off with one another and see who wins the day.'

'Sorry,' Vin said, 'Hutch is no match for you, and I don't think I could take you and your brother both. But I can tell you, the death knell has sounded – everyone in Rio Blanco is going to die.'

'So we fight,' Dean said from a few feet away. 'And your gang – even should they win – will leave with very few men left alive.'

'What about me?' Vin asked. 'You just going to execute me, or is there a man among you who has the guts to try me on – fair and square?'

Charo held up his hand to silence Dean and Trace's objections before they cold be raised.

'You didn't just come to count our number; you came to find me.'

Vin grinned. 'You're supposed to be something of a specialist with a gun. Well, I live for good times and excitement. The good times I have after we raid a settlement or sell a herd of stolen beef. I like to spend money, drink, gamble and chase a few skirts. For excitement, I like to find a man with guts, guts enough to face me with a gun. You live for cows, kids, a family and a home. I live for the thrills I get. It's that simple.'

'You could have had the thrill and excitement that first day,' Trace told him. 'The eight of you could probably have taken the town. There were only a couple of men wearing guns, and I'm handier with a rifle than a handgun. Why didn't you do it?'

'Yeah, we could have done it,' Vin admitted, 'but I wanted to meet the man who put out the candles. I'm a very good shot, but I couldn't do that trick.' He scoffed. 'Of course, candles don't shoot back.'

'Neither does a man who comes in second on a fast draw,' Charo commented.

Vin snorted his contempt. 'Only one way to prove who's the slower one.'

Charo took out his right-hand gun. He carefully emptied it, then put one back in the chamber.

'Give him one bullet,' Charo told Trace.

'You don't have to prove anything,' Trace told his brother. 'This man's a murderer, a rustler and a bandit. He doesn't deserve anything more than a noose around his neck.'

Charo shook out his shoulders and stretched a little to wake up his muscles. 'Do it,' he said calmly. 'Hate to cheat this murdering scum out of a chance to walk free.'

Trace removed all but one of the cartridges and stuck the gun back in Vin's holster.

'It's ready to shoot,' he told the gunman.

Charo spun the cylinder of his gun, adjusting it so the hammer would fall on the single round. He then holstered the gun and put his back to the wall. Vin was standing opposite with a wall at his back as well.

'A man can teach himself to be fast,' Charo remarked to Vin, 'but speed isn't what kills – it's accuracy. You've only got one bullet, so you can't miss your mark. If you get me first but don't kill me, then, sure as we're standing here in the same barn, I'll kill you.'

'We ought to use a rope and hang him,' Dean spoke up. 'This is crazy, Charo!'

Lacy looked around in amazement. 'You mean it … just you and me?'

'You win – you walk away. That ought to be simple enough for even a cold-blooded coyote like you to understand.'

Vin licked his lips, his eyes darting about, wondering if this was on the level. No one else was pointing their weapon at him now. All he had to do was defeat Charo. It's what he had wanted.

'Remember what I said,' Charo warned him. 'You only have one shot. If you miss, you're dead. I might not be as quick as you, but I never miss what I aim at.'

The statement caused beads of sweat to appear on Vin's brow. He'd killed several other men, but he always made sure of his kill. The fight he bragged about – killing Larry Dilts at Fort Worth – had been face-to-face, but he'd shot the man three times. He wasn't sure which bullet even killed him, just that he'd shot him first and continued to fire until he went down. This was different. He had to make certain of his one shot. It had to be perfect.

'When I drop my hat,' Trace made the announcement, standing off to the side, halfway between the two men. He pulled his wide-brimmed hat from his head and held it out in front of him. He paused to look at each man … then dropped it!

Charo's hand was quicker than the naked eye could see, his motion fluid and practiced. Vin matched his draw almost exactly, but Vin had to make certain of his shot – Charo knew his shot would be true.

Vin lost a micro-second to aim. But, as his finger tightened on the trigger, a lead pellet tore through his chest. The force caused him to jerk slightly forward, and he lost his chance to shoot.

Vin staggered back a step and fought to regain his balance, but his arm could no longer support the weight of his gun. It fell harmlessly to the floor at his feet. Next, the straw strewn floor rushed up to slam him in the face. He neither saw it nor felt it.

Before anyone could react, a second gunshot came from the loft. 'I hit him!' Randy's voice called out. 'There were two of them!'

Trace checked outside the door and moved a few feet so he could look up at Randy. 'Which way?'

'Headed past the barricade,' Randy called down. 'I think I hit him pretty good.'

Trace found the man's footprints in the dusty street, along with a few drops of blood. He knelt down and lit a match, to get an idea of how badly the man was hit. Sometimes a bit of blood would have foam in it, indicating a bullet through the lung. He could see nothing from the blood trail, but he did recognize the footprints. Moccasins.

'He's gone!' he called back, looking around carefully, before returning to the barn.

'What do you think?' Charo asked, as he fed bullets into his right-hand gun.

'I think it must have been the Indian. He could have been watching the whole time, getting an exact count of our guns.'

'But he didn't see Randy,' Dean said. 'With his leg wound, he has been keeping watch from the loft.'

'We're thinning them down,' Charo said. 'Amando, the renegade

Indians, Dutch Eller, Vin Lacy ... and now the bandit Indian.' He allowed a bit of optimism to enter his voice. 'If they keep coming at us a man or two at time, we'll win this here fight easy.'

'After you taking Vin, no one is going to offer another straight-out gunfight,' Trace told him.

'I never knew you were so quick,' Dean praised him. 'I thought you were crazy to give the man a chance to kill you and walk away.'

Charo looked at Trace, and Trace said: 'Actually, Charo had his fingers crossed when he said that. If Vin had killed Charo, I'd have shot him on the spot.'

'I'm glad you didn't have to take a hand in it,' Dean said. 'Good shooting, Charo.'

***

Hutch Eller knelt down over Cuerdo. The Indian had both hands over his wound, but there was nothing to be done for him. He told them about Vin and Charo's gunfight, about how there were still eight or ten fighting men, then how he'd been spotted after Vin lost the fight.

Enrico stood at Eller's back, listening to the report. The words stopped after a few sentences and Cuerdo spoke no more. He was gone.

'We should have never come to Rio Blanco,' Enrico said. 'We rode into this valley with a small army. Now we are too few to win a battle against a farm house.'

Hutch stood up, his fists balled at his sides, face near black with fury. 'Tomorrow they all die!' he roared. 'Everyone get some sleep. We leave at first light and don't quit until we've destroyed the town and everyone in it!'

'But the McCains are still there,' Enrico contended. 'They are crack shots and have already cut us to pieces!'

'Everyone dies!' Hutch snarled the order. 'Put out a guard or two and get some sleep. Tomorrow we put an end to the McCains ... and the whole damn town!'

Chapter Eleven

With the probability of this being the last night of their lives, Melanie went to sleep in Trace's arms, nestled in a corner of the hayloft. A couple hours before daylight, he awoke for his turn on guard duty. When he tried to ease out without waking her, Melanie tightened her small fists in the fold of his shirt.

'Don't go,' she whispered, still half asleep.

'I've got to take my turn on watch he told her quietly, attempting to remove her firm grip.

'Just a little longer,' she implored him, still with her eyes closed.

'Look, kitten,' he pleaded. 'I've got to relieve Charo at the store. We only have two men on watch.'

The eyes fluttered open, Melanie's face looking very small and delicate in the subdue light. She sat up, allowing Trace to do the same.

'Was this our last night together, Trace?' she barely breathed the words. 'Will we all die today?'

Trace put a hand on her shoulder and squeezed gently.

'We'll make it, Melanie. We've got too much to live for to give it all up.'

She smiled weakly. 'Like the house you might build for us, overlooking the river – where we first met?'

He grinned, enjoying the warmth in her expression, the sincere tone of her voice, and just being close to her.

'I've been promising myself that I'd tell you something – I've been meaning to say it for some time.'

'What's that?'

He took a deep breath, wondering why it took more strength to say something nice to a woman than it took to fight a man the size of Lex Banning.

'I've been wanting to tell you that I – I love you, Melanie,' he stammered.

Her eyes brightened and a slender simper played on her lips. 'I didn't think you'd ever get up the gumption to tell me – not outright.' She laughed. 'My big strong man of few words.'

'I didn't want you thinking – '

She put two fingers to his lips – much the same as the night after the dance. 'A few words are all it takes, Trace … as long as they are the words I've been wanting to hear.'

He kissed her on the lips, then left her in the warm bit of hay. Something in his chest grew, an inner strength that prompted him to a new readiness. He felt invulnerable, empowered by an unseen force. Love for Melanie gave him a new motivation. Let Hutch Eller come! Let him bring his twenty or more men! He would cut them down as fast as he could pull the trigger. Nothing was going to prevent him from living his dream. Nothing could –

Trace stopped as he reached the main floor. The parson, the sheriff, the storekeeper … every man left able to stand were there to confront him. He didn't know what was up, so he put a puzzled look on each man.

'We've got something to say to you, Trace McCain,' Barney spoke up.

The others gathered around. Trace wondered what was up, being joined by Dean and Charo in the middle of the barn. Everyone had come in for this impromptu meeting. He looked to his brothers, but they also appeared perplexed as to what was going on.

'We would all like to express our thanks to your family,' Lyle Tibbs said from his bed in one corner of the room.

'That's right,' Doc Myer agreed. 'We've done you boys wrong ever since your pa – well, we blamed you for his sins. Having gotten to know you personally, we can see how you boys were also victims of your father's transgressions. Sometimes we forget that kids don't ask to be born to a man like John McCain. And we can see now that he was the only bad apple in your entire family.'

'Doc's telling it straight,' Barney took over. 'I admit I was one of them who held a grudge for Randolph's death. He was a well-thought-of man, one we all knew, liked and respected. Your pa ... well, we had the opposite opinion of him.' He shook his head. 'But we shouldn't have taken it out on you boys.'

'We know you fellows didn't have to come here to town,' the parson took over. 'You could have been safely back at the fortress of your own home. Yet you chose to side us in this fight.'

'Not to mention, you're the best fighters we have,' Barney admitted.

'We're saying, we're proud to have you stand with us – ' the parson looked at the three of them – each and every one of you. Without you boys, we'd have been wiped out on the first attack.'

Trace looked at the people around him. They were beaten, prepared for the final battle that might end all of their lives. They wanted to clear their consciences and make amends. The faces were mixed with two readable emotions – fear and regret.

'We've been telling you a long time that Rio Blanco is our home,' Trace reminded them. 'What kind of neighbors would we be if we had stood back and watched some lowdown buzzards burn it to the ground?'

'We wanted to clear the air,' Doc Myer spoke up again. 'It's a privilege and an honor to face this last battle with you men at our side.'

'We ain't dead yet,' Charo said. 'There can't be more than fifteen or twenty of those losers left.' He waved his hand in a show of confidence.

'Why, hell. They would need twice that many to finish us off.'

'Especially when you've got help those bandits don't know about!' came a strong, familiar voice from the front door.

Trace recognized the man speaking at once, relief washing over him like a warm blanket. There was only one man in the country with a deep, ragged voice such as that – Sod McCain!

The head of the McCain family wandered into the light, and trailing behind were six men – rough, hardened men. Two of them still wore their gray Rebel caps. Trace, Dean, and Charo gathered around their grandfather at once, greeting him with warm shakes of the hand and pats on his back.

'Lucky for you people we weren't the bandit gang,' Sod remarked. 'We could have swept in here and caught you all napping.' He frowned. 'Where are your night guards?'

'Randy must have fallen asleep,' the parson said. 'He's up in the loft.'

Sod's expression showed his worry. 'What about the Circle M?'

'Bud was hit pretty hard, but he seems to be getting better. We lost Stoco and a couple other hired men. Lonnie is out at the ranch with Tish Banning, Lora and Ma. We can only hope Eller doesn't try our place a second time, while we're all here in town.'

'From all of the bullet holes and broken windows along the main street, it must have been a real war.'

'We've had our hands full,' Trace admitted.

Sod introduced his six men quickly, then turned to the chore at hand.

'We met the Myers' kid a day's ride from here.' As Doc looked around swiftly for his boy, Sod went on with his story. 'He'd ridden his horse to death and been walking and running for two days. We left him at a trading post to get some rest and road all night to get back here.'

'We're glad you made it back,' Dean said. 'We thought it might take a couple of days to round up enough men to make the trip worthwhile.'

'I couldn't raise a single man in town, so I paid these men's fines. They were jailed after getting into a brawl with some ex-Yankee troopers. I told them what we're up against and offered to hire them all – either to work for us, or I thought Kendall could use a few.' He looked around. 'Harvey isn't here?'

Trace explained about the fate of their ranch and finished with: 'I'm sure Randy will hire all of these men.'

'We ain't earned nothing yet,' one of the men spoke up. 'My sister lived in Little Bend. I got word her family had to skedaddle or be killed when this same band of marauders hit. They destroyed their house by fire when they left. I'm looking for some payback.'

Trace suddenly had an idea. 'I think that's a fine idea.'

Everyone in the place turned to look at him, so he quickly told them his plan.

Charo was the first to agree by saying: 'Now you're singing my kind of tune.'

***

As the first inkling of daylight cracked the dark eastern sky, Trace let the way forward. The other men spread out and waited a short way off, barely visible in the early morning gloom. He was worried about not finding a sentry or two. Surely, Hutch would put out guards. He had to know the townspeople might stage a last-ditch raid of some kind to save Rio Blanco from being burned to the ground. Was it possible they had moved the camp? Could they be on their way to attack the nearly unarmed town?

Easing quietly along the trail, he reached the encampment. The fire pit was cold, and there wasn't a soul to be seen – other than a lone body lying next to his saddle and ground blanket.

He signaled to the others to come ahead and was inspecting the dead man as they rode up.

'Big man, red hair, a short beard – if I'm not mistaken, this is Hutch Eller,' Trace announced. 'I got off a quick shot at another man about his size and coloring. I don't know how hard I hit him, but he fit the description of one of the Ellers.'

Charo inspected the body and did a quick search. 'No saddlebags, no money belt – his pockets have been picked clean.'

'Yes, someone cut his throat,' Trace said. 'I'd say the other men were in disagreement about attacking the town again.'

'Funny,' Charo pointed out. 'We all thought Rio Blanco would be our last stand. Turns out, it was the last stand of Eller's Marauders.'

'I'd say you are right,' Dean observed. 'Other than several graves, there's not another rider in sight.'

'Too bad,' the one ex-rebel said. 'We could have taken them by surprise and eliminated them all.'

'Might have been a couple who got away in the fighting anyway,' Dean said. 'They are without a leader, broken into groups of two or three. They'll all meet their end soon enough.'

'What now?' Charo asked.

'We go home,' Dean said. 'You boys can talk to Randy about working for him. He lost his entire crew, so he should be offering top-hand wages.'

'Reckon we can tend a few cattle,' the Reb replied. 'Our last job was on a cattle drive. About the only work we could find since the war. Most of us have been drifting except for that.'

'Be nice to belong again,' said one of the others.

'If Randy doesn't take you all, we've got a spot for you at the McCain ranch,' Dean told them.

'Any volunteers to bury this mongrel?' Trace tossed out the query. 'I'll help, but I don't aim to dig that large of hole by myself.'

Charo shook his head. 'Ain't no one waiting for me to come back,

Trace. You head on back to your sweetheart. Me and a couple of these new volunteers can handle a burying.'

'You're going to work so I can get back to my girl?' Trace was incredulous. 'What's gotten into you?'

Charo grinned. 'You wouldn't be worth your salt, thinking of Melanie pacing the barn, wondering if she'll ever see you again. That gal would scald my hide if I returned without you in tow.' He grunted his disdain. 'Darned if you ain't as bad as a married man already.'

Trace laughed. 'Best get used to it. There will be a wedding coming up right sudden.'

'I can hardly wait,' Charo said, displaying disgust. 'Next thing, there will be a host of little ones running all over the ranch. Be like having mice and no cats.'

Dean pointed a warning finger at Charo. 'We haven't said anything yet, but Lora is with child. You go comparing our baby to a mouse and you'll be fixing your own meals.'

'Great!' Charo grumbled. 'With Lonnie tying the knot, me and Bud are going to outnumbered by married men in the family. What a life that's going to be.'

'Yes,' Trace agreed happily. 'What a life indeed!'

END

ABOUT THE AUTHOR

Terrell L Bowers grew up playing cowboys, with his own horse and guns. His father got him to reading Westerns after he'd finished high school and, after a couple hundred titles, he began writing his own stories. Took him fifteen years before he found a receptive editor. Since that time, he has had over 40 titles published in the US and more than 30 titles published in the UK. He writes action, romance and humor in his stories, without the use of sex, gore or profanity. He is married, with two daughters and one grandchild.

Printed in the USA
CPSIA information can be obtained
at www.ICGtesting.com
LVHW020432040924
789995LV00002B/348

9 781541 076365